MR. BADGER AND MRS. FOX #4

PEACE AND QUIET

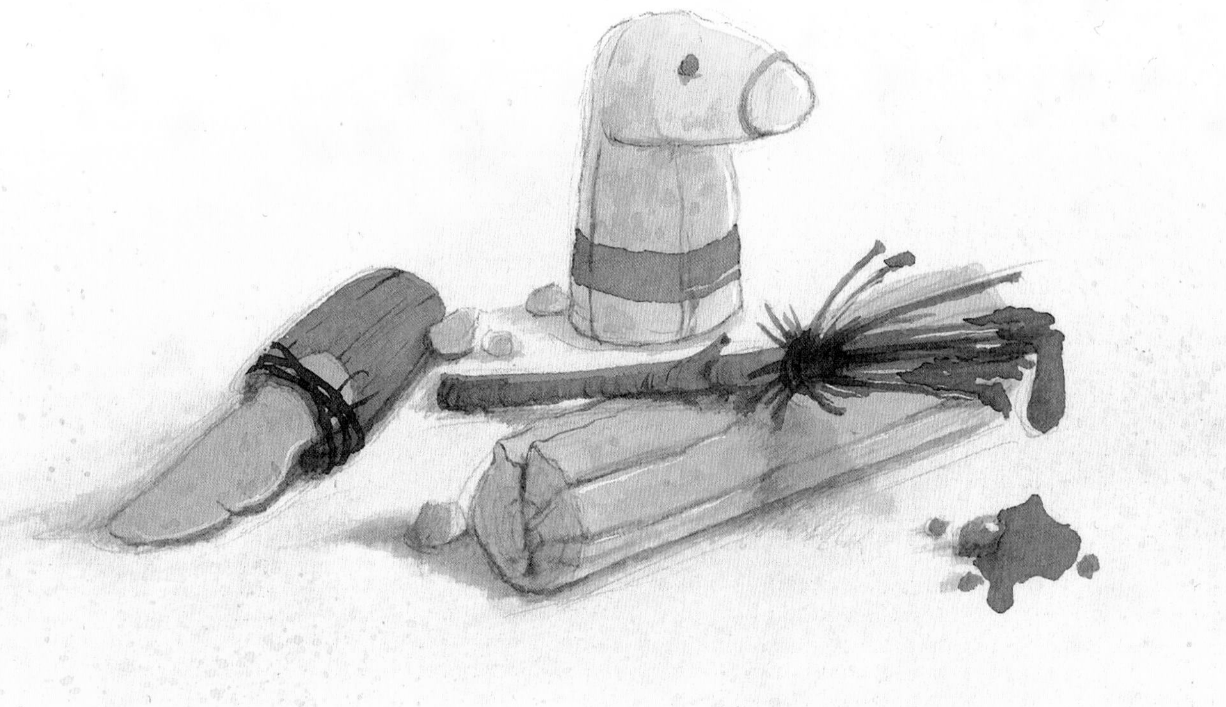

Brigitte LUCIANI & Eve THARLET

Graphic Universe™ • Minneapolis • New York

For Louise and Loly, for summertime friends . . .
—E.T.

Story by Brigitte Luciani
Art by Eve Tharlet
Translation by Carol Klio Burrell

First American edition published in 2012 by Graphic Universe™.
Published by arrangement with MEDIATOON LICENSING - France.

Monsieur Blaireau et Madame Renarde
4/Jamais tranquille!
© DARGAUD 2010 - Tharlet & Luciani
www.dargaud.com

Graphic Universe™
A division of Lerner Publishing Group, Inc.
241 First Avenue North
Minneapolis, MN 55401 U.S.A.

Website address: www.lernerbooks.com

Library of Congress Cataloging-in-Publication Data

Luciani, Brigitte.
[Jamais tranquille! English]
Peace and quiet / by Brigitte Luciani ; illustrated by Eve Tharlet.
p.   cm. — (Mr. Badger and Mrs. Fox ; 4)
Summary: Despite their different habits, Mr. Badger and Mrs. Fox
get their blended family ready for winter.
ISBN 978-0-7613-8520-2 (lib. bdg. : alk. paper)
1. Graphic novels. [1. Graphic novels. 2. Stepfamilies—Fiction. 3. Brothers and sisters—
Fiction. 4. Badgers—Fiction. 5. Foxes—Fiction. 6. Winter—Fiction.] I. Tharlet, Eve, ill. II. Title.
PZ7.7.L83Pe 2012
741.5'944—dc23   2011049904

Manufactured in the United States of America
1 - DP - 7/15/12

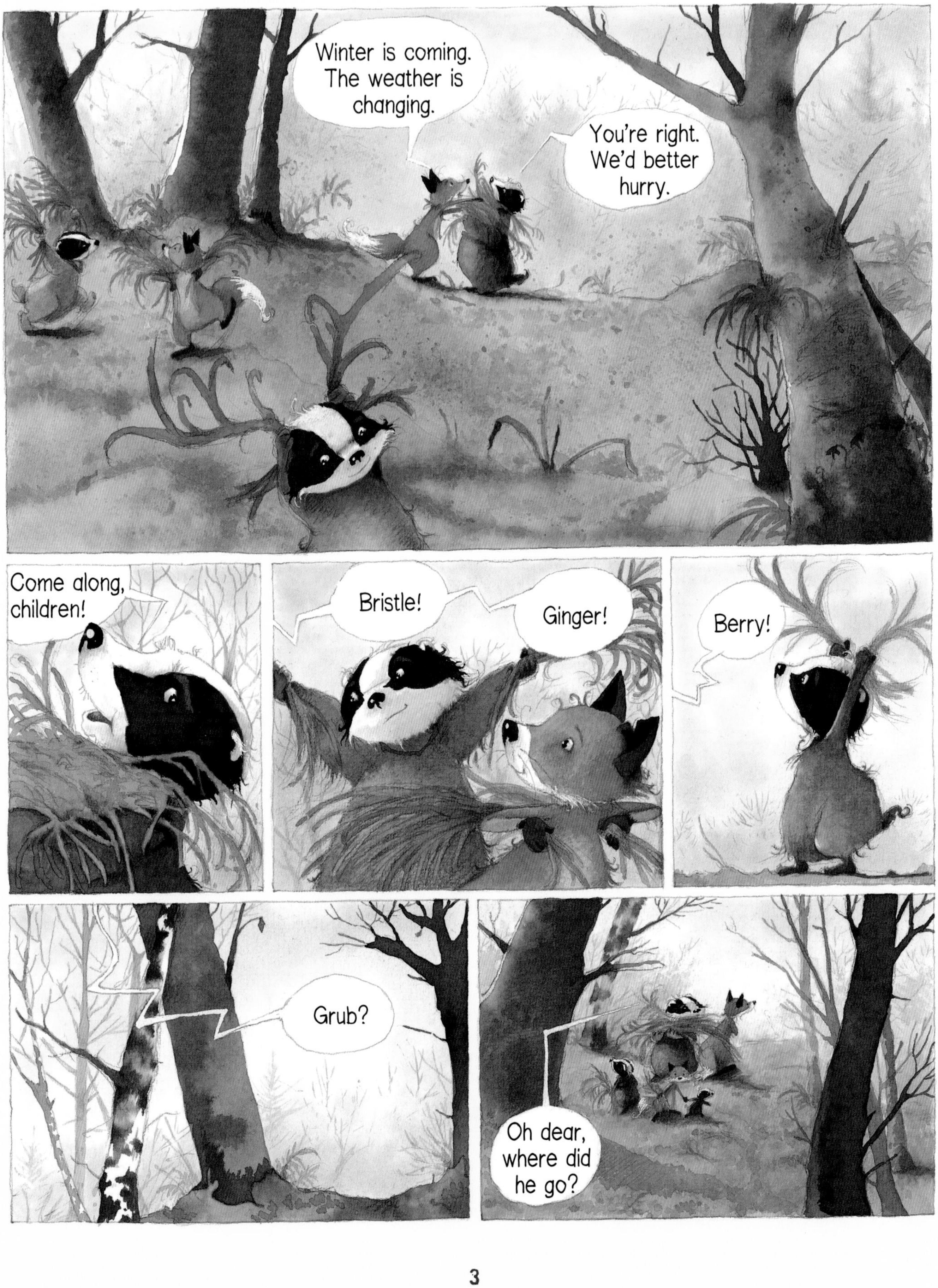
Winter is coming. The weather is changing.
You're right. We'd better hurry.
Come along, children!
Bristle!
Ginger!
Berry!
Grub?
Oh dear, where did he go?

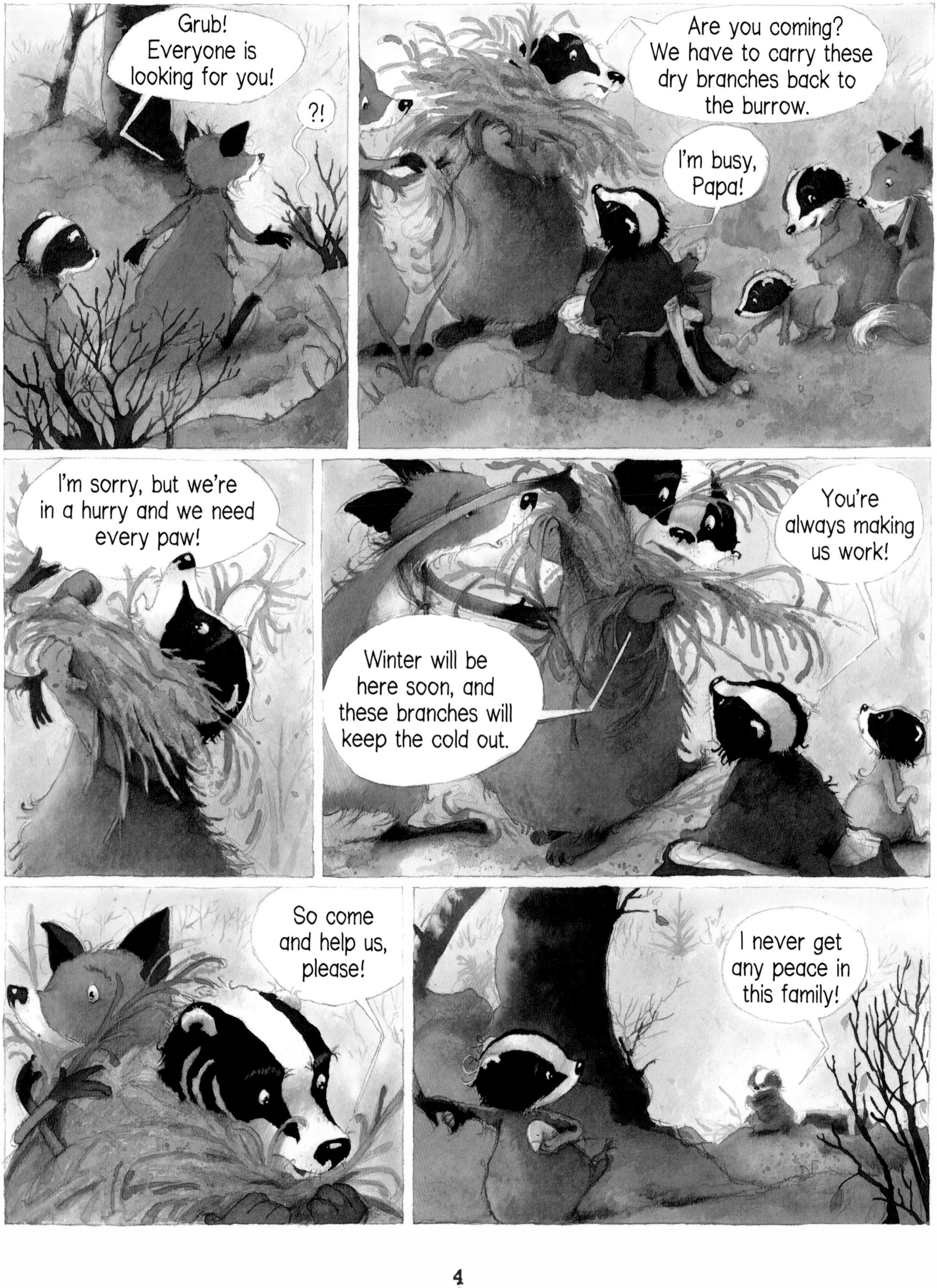
Grub! Everyone is looking for you!
?!
Are you coming? We have to carry these dry branches back to the burrow.
I'm busy, Papa!
I'm sorry, but we're in a hurry and we need every paw!
You're always making us work!
Winter will be here soon, and these branches will keep the cold out.
So come and help us, please!
I never get any peace in this family!

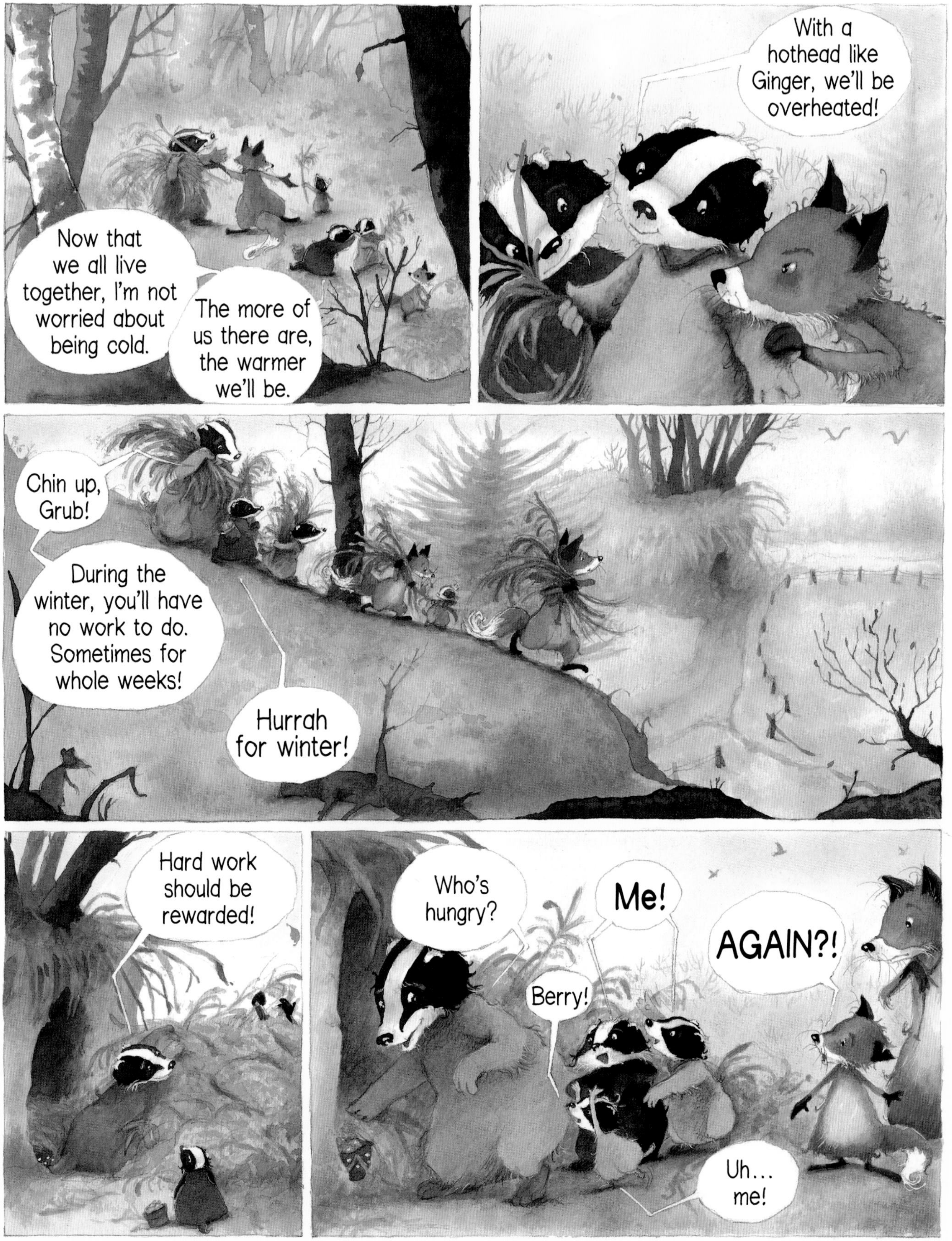
Now that we all live together, I'm not worried about being cold.
The more of us there are, the warmer we'll be.
With a hothead like Ginger, we'll be overheated!
Chin up, Grub!
During the winter, you'll have no work to do. Sometimes for whole weeks!
Hurrah for winter!
Hard work should be rewarded!
Who's hungry?
Me!
Berry!
AGAIN?!
Uh... me!

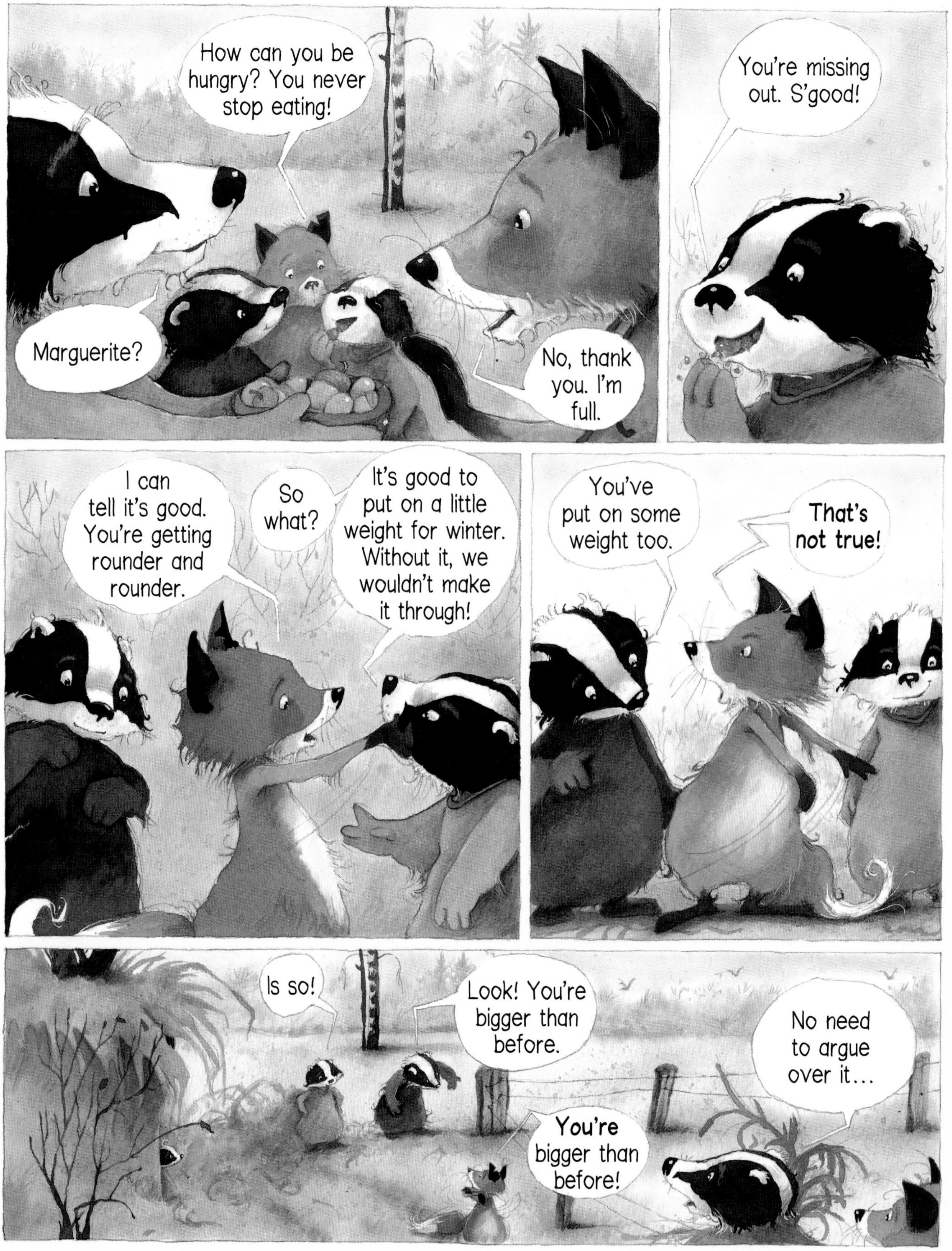
How can you be hungry? You never stop eating!
Marguerite?
No, thank you. I'm full.
You're missing out. S'good!
I can tell it's good. You're getting rounder and rounder.
So what?
It's good to put on a little weight for winter. Without it, we wouldn't make it through!
You've put on some weight too.
That's not true!
Is so!
Look! You're bigger than before.
You're bigger than before!
No need to argue over it…

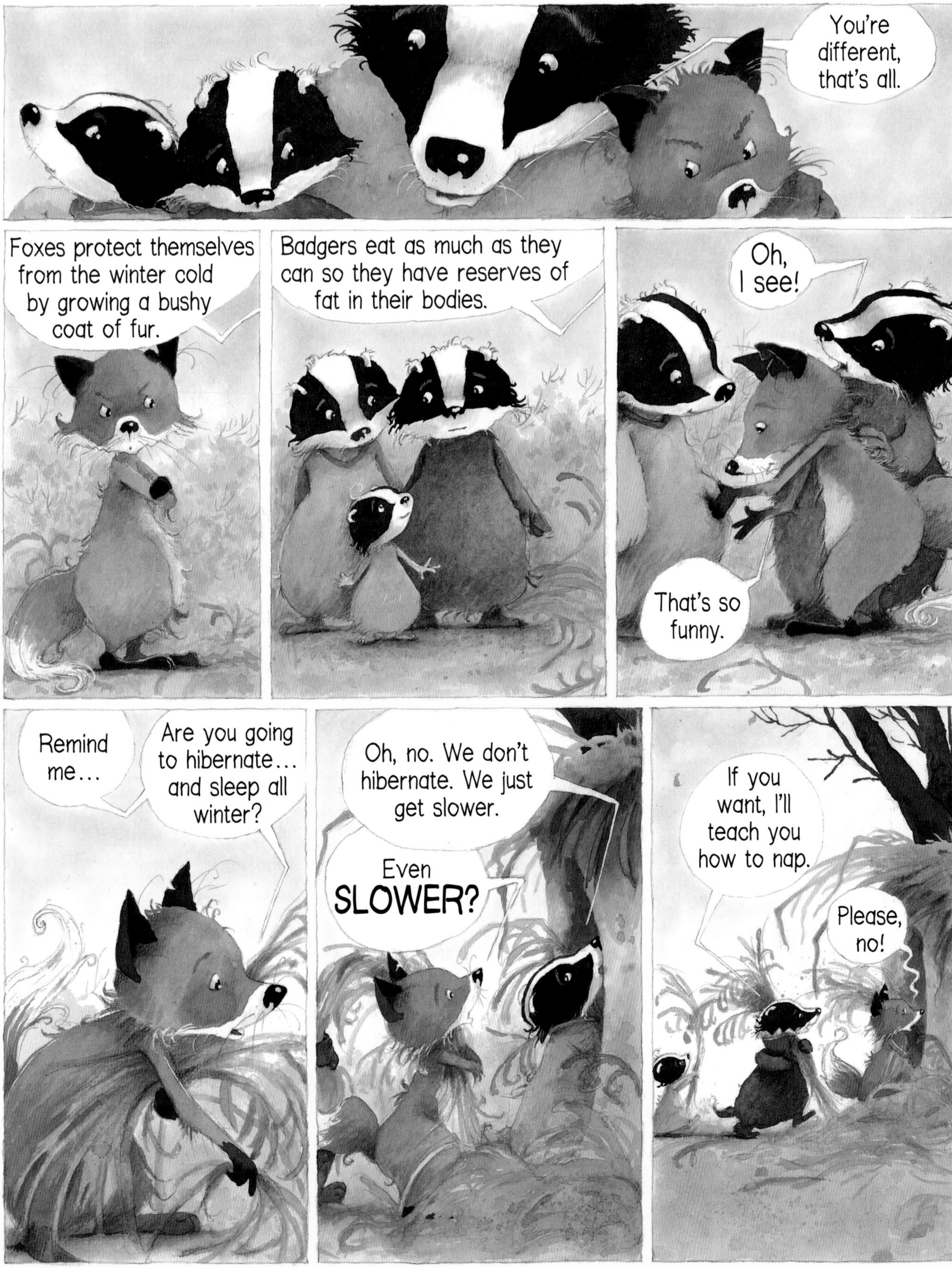
You're different, that's all.
Foxes protect themselves from the winter cold by growing a bushy coat of fur.
Badgers eat as much as they can so they have reserves of fat in their bodies.
Oh, I see!
That's so funny.
Remind me…
Are you going to hibernate… and sleep all winter?
Oh, no. We don't hibernate. We just get slower.
Even SLOWER?
If you want, I'll teach you how to nap.
Please, no!

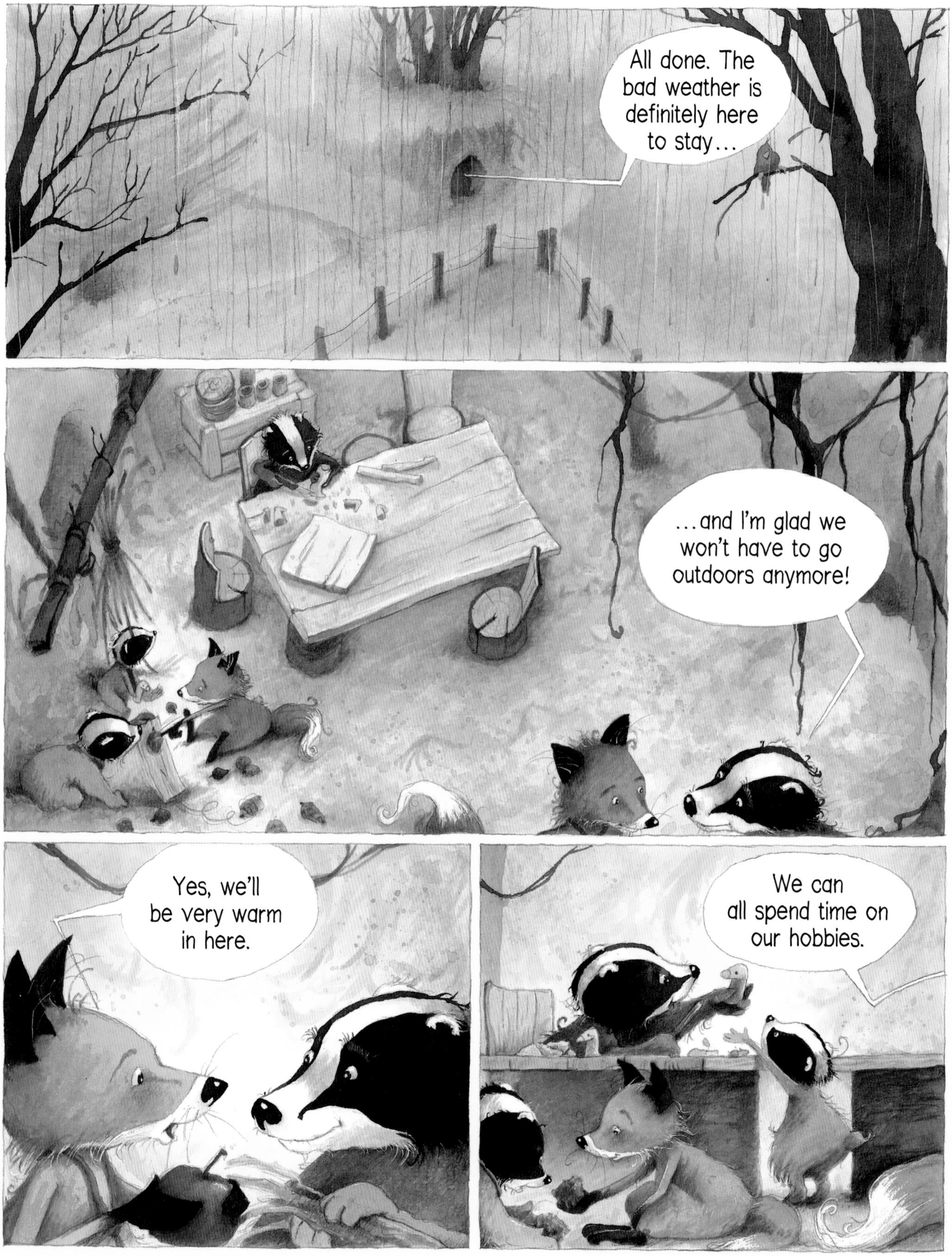
All done. The bad weather is definitely here to stay...
...and I'm glad we won't have to go outdoors anymore!
Yes, we'll be very warm in here.
We can all spend time on our hobbies.

But since we're all cooped up in here together, things might get less peaceful soon...

Don't worry. We always just sleep a lot.

You, maybe. But not us!

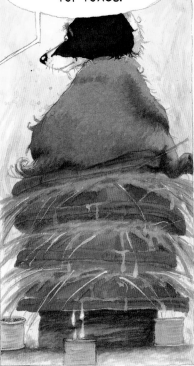

Winter is **anything but** a time to rest for foxes.

Then just enjoy this moment of quiet!

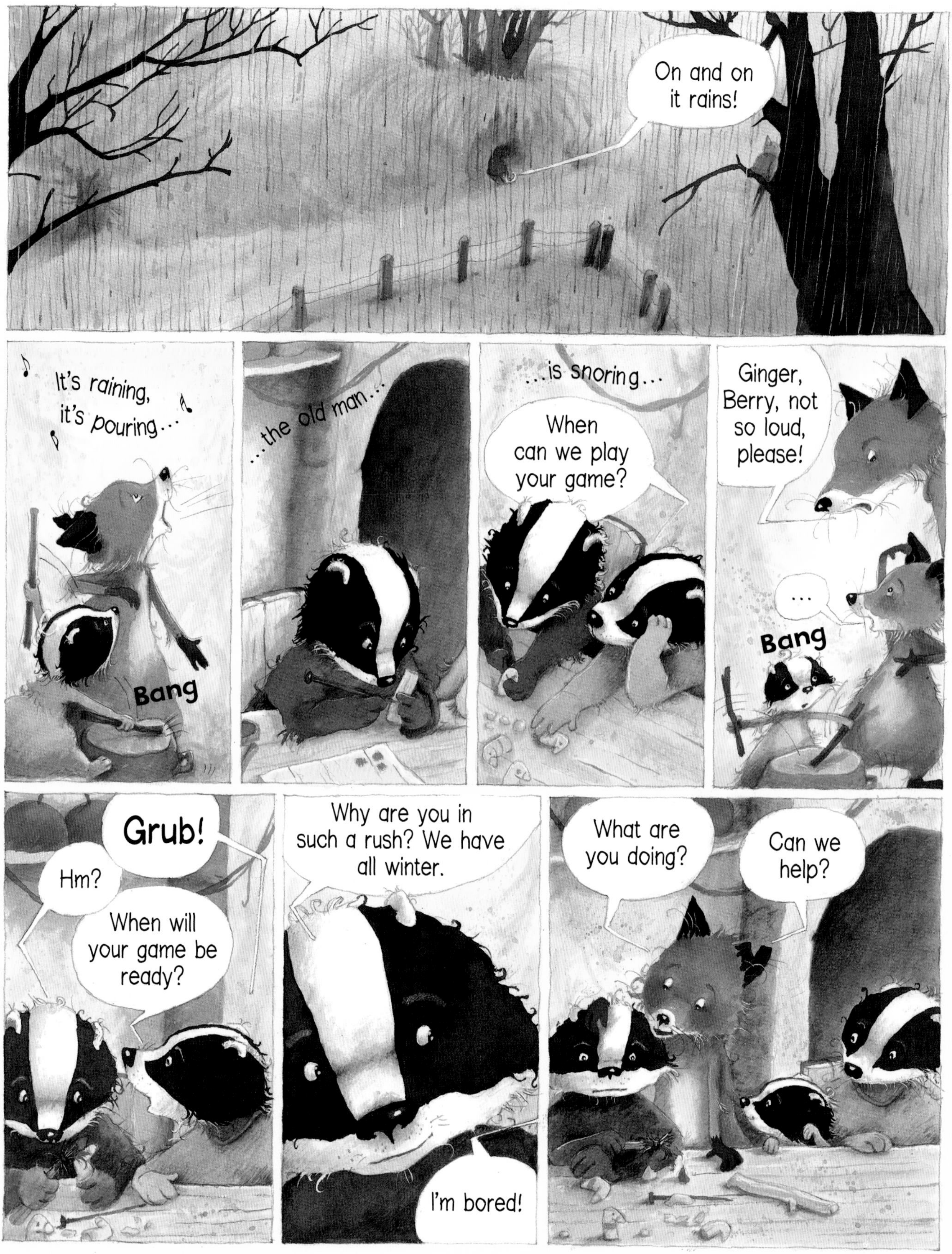
On and on it rains!
It's raining, it's pouring...
Bang
...the old man...
...is snoring...
When can we play your game?
Ginger, Berry, not so loud, please!
...
Bang
Grub!
Hm?
When will your game be ready?
Why are you in such a rush? We have all winter.
I'm bored!
What are you doing?
Can we help?

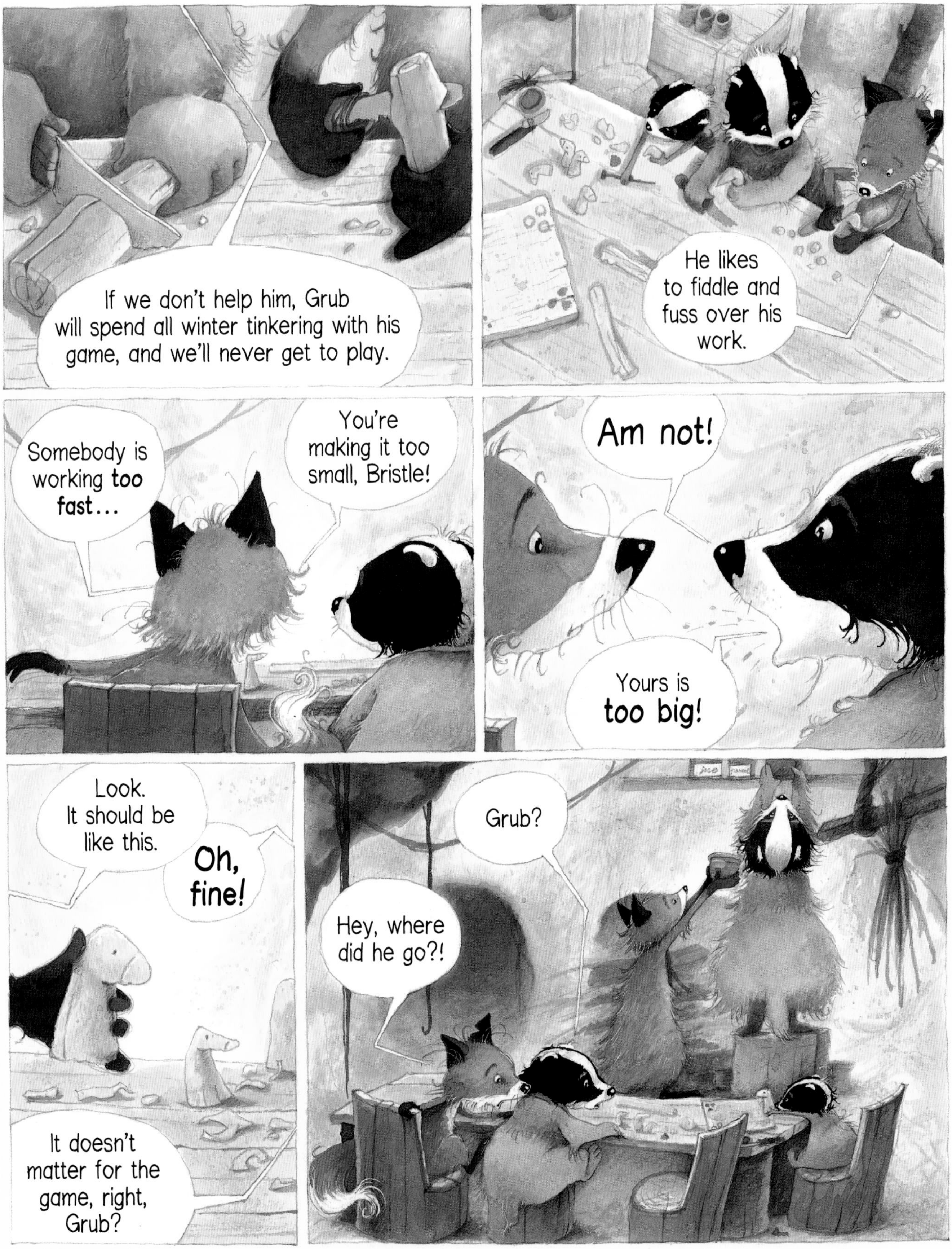
If we don't help him, Grub will spend all winter tinkering with his game, and we'll never get to play.
He likes to fiddle and fuss over his work.
Somebody is working **too fast**...
You're making it too small, Bristle!
Am not!
Yours is **too big!**
Look. It should be like this.
Oh, fine!
It doesn't matter for the game, right, Grub?
Grub?
Hey, where did he go?!

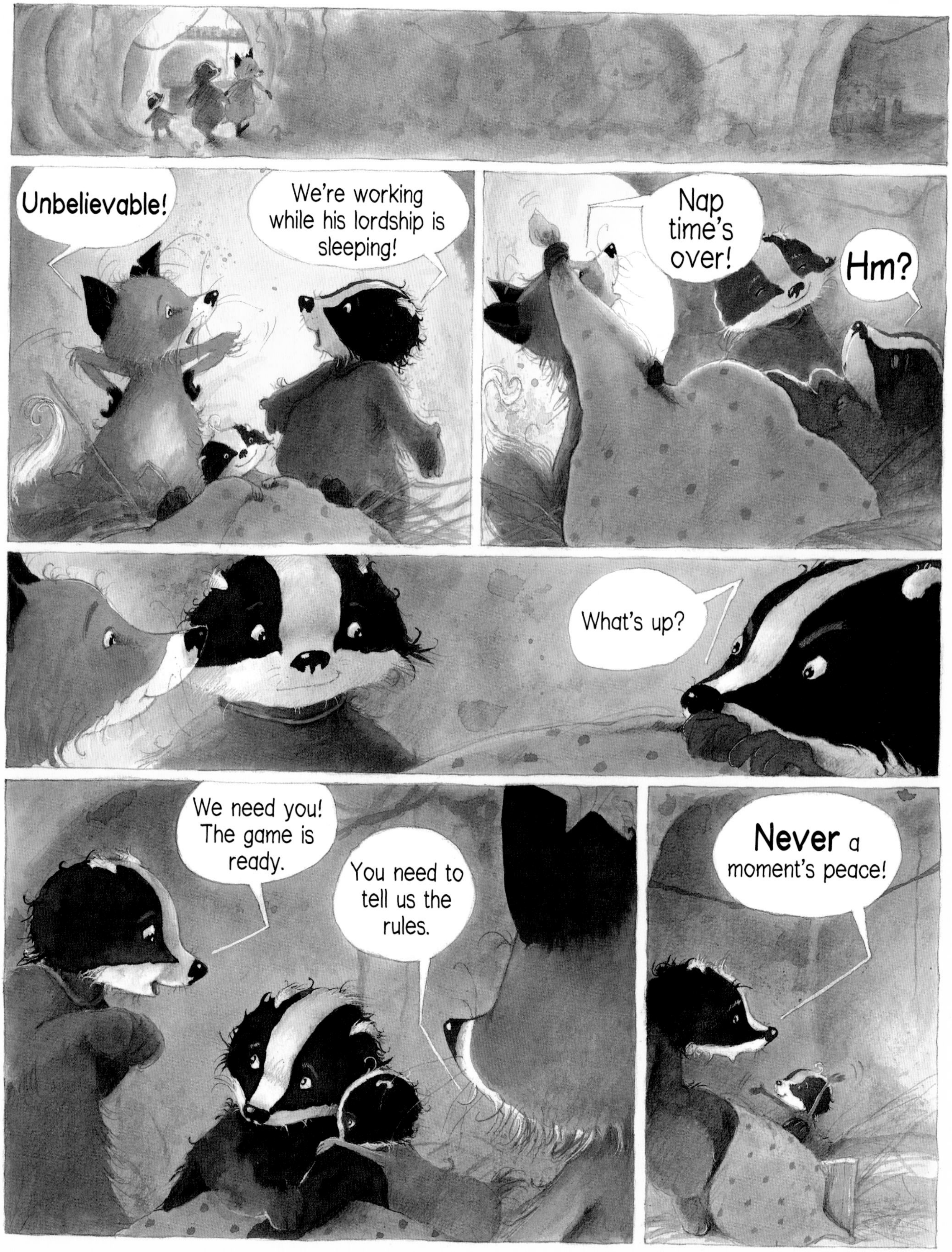
Unbelievable!
We're working while his lordship is sleeping!
Nap time's over!
Hm?
What's up?
We need you! The game is ready.
You need to tell us the rules.
Never a moment's peace!

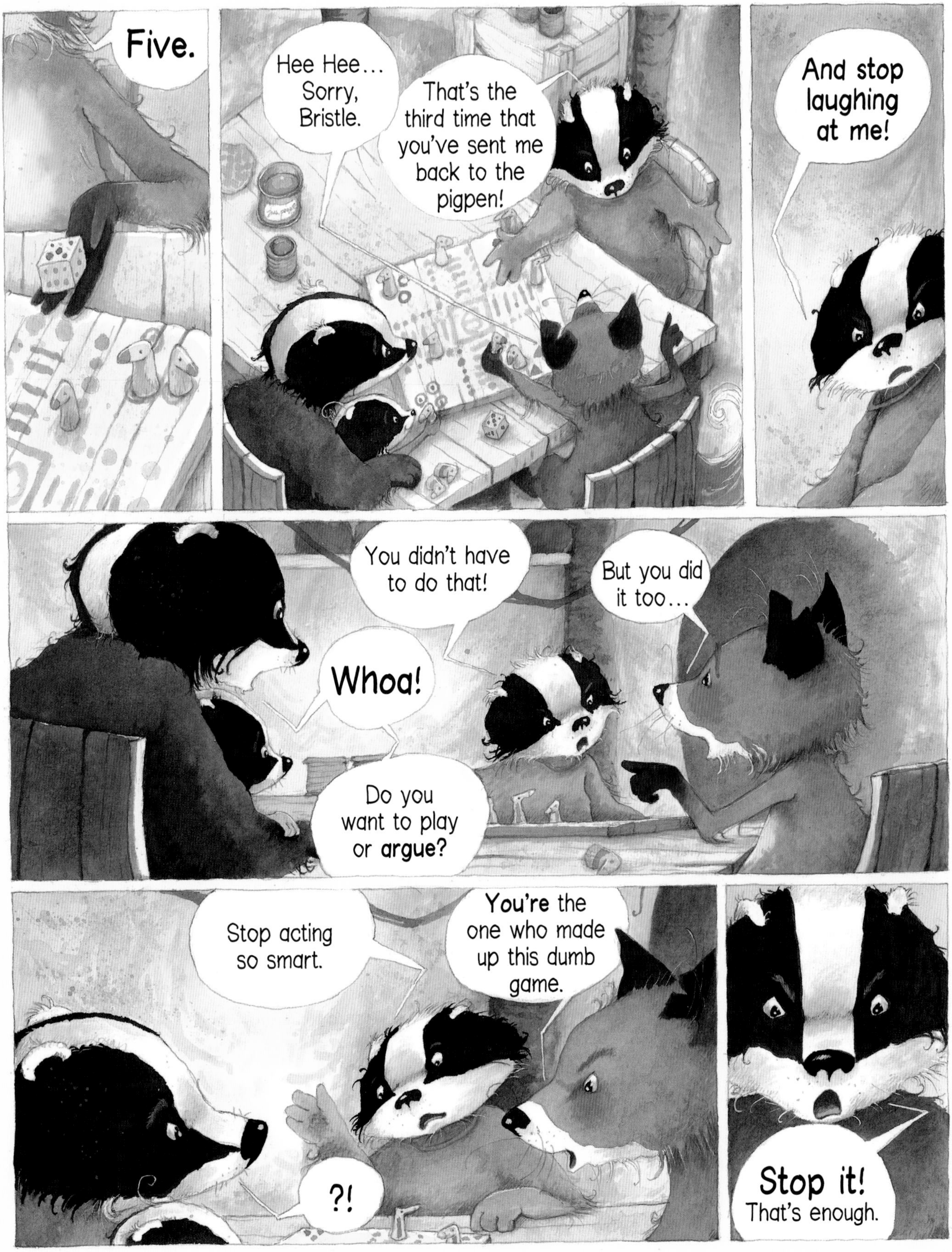
Five.
Hee Hee... Sorry, Bristle.
That's the third time that you've sent me back to the pigpen!
And stop laughing at me!
You didn't have to do that!
But you did it too...
Whoa!
Do you want to play or **argue**?
Stop acting so smart.
You're the one who made up this dumb game.
?!
Stop it! That's enough.

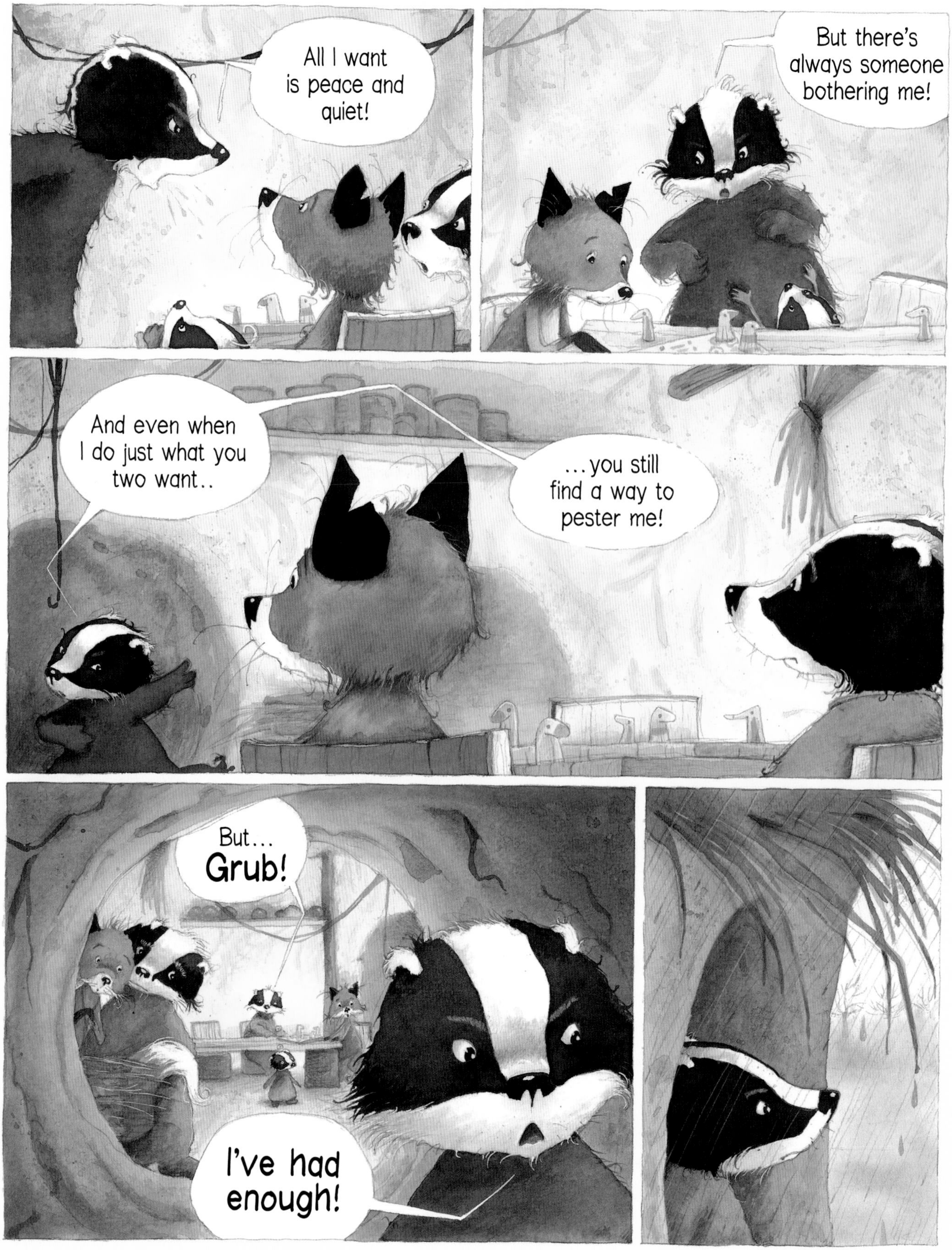
All I want is peace and quiet!
But there's always someone bothering me!
And even when I do just what you two want..
...you still find a way to pester me!
But... Grub!
I've had enough!

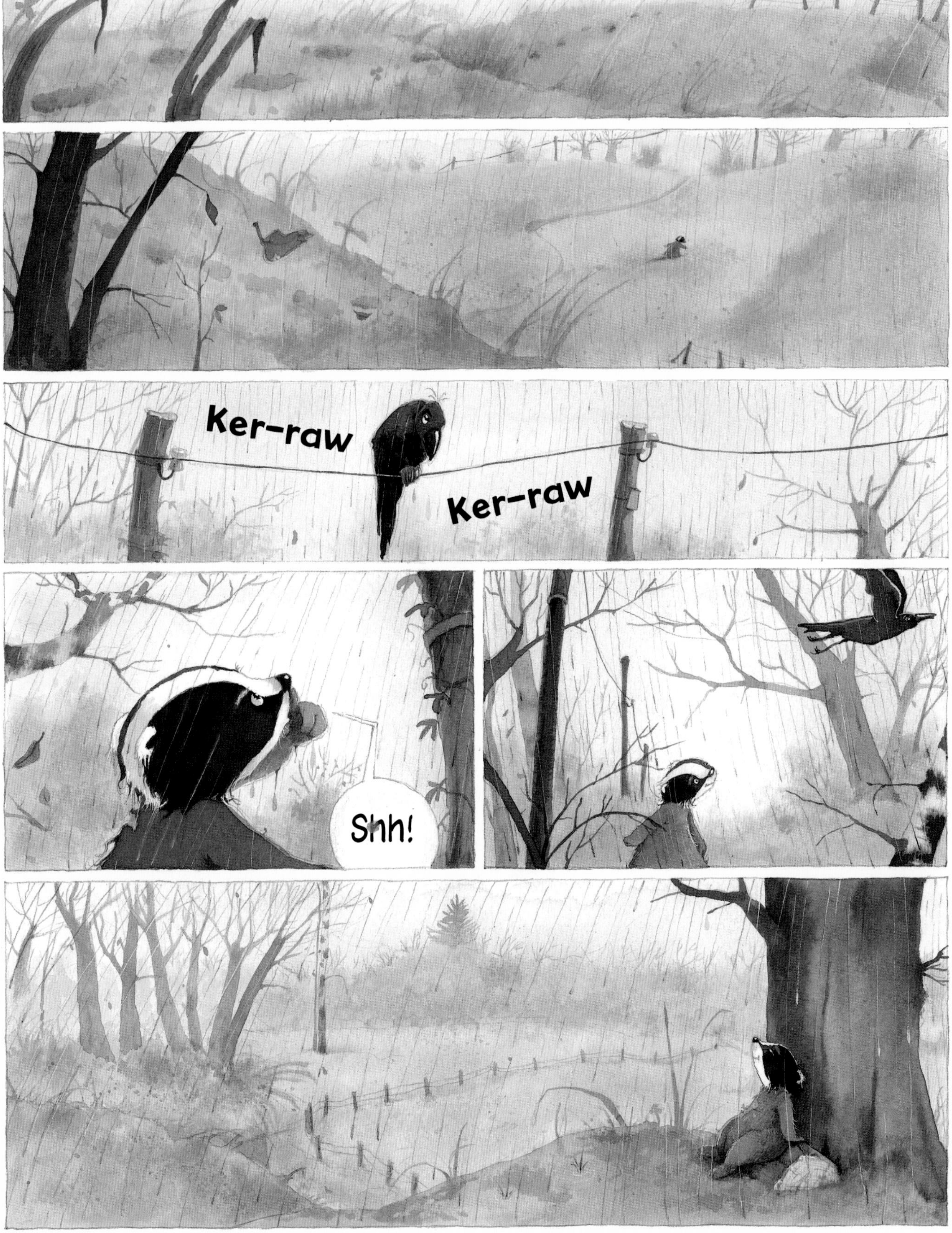
Ker-raw
Ker-raw
Shh!

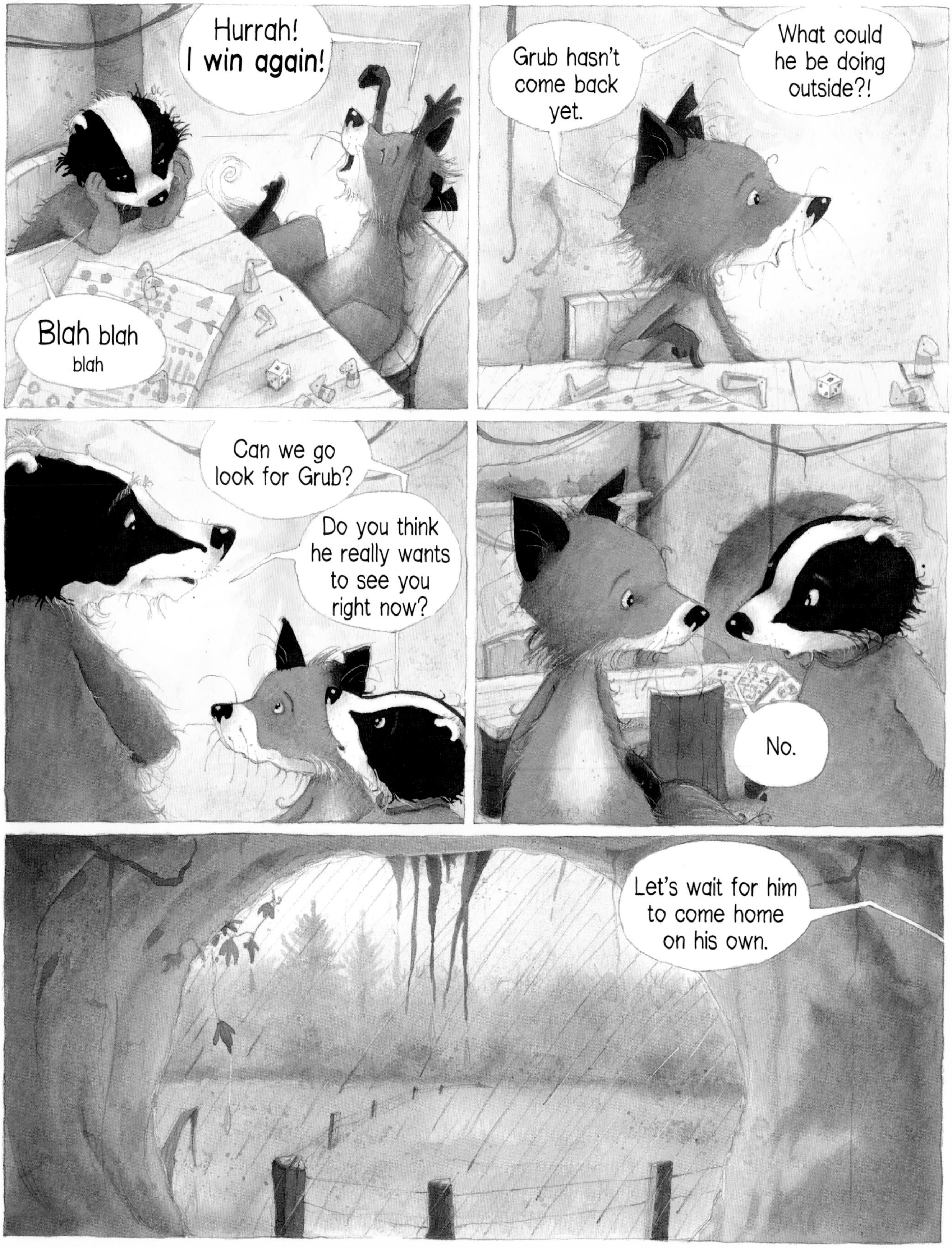
Hurrah! I win again!
Blah blah blah
Grub hasn't come back yet.
What could he be doing outside?!
Can we go look for Grub?
Do you think he really wants to see you right now?
No.
Let's wait for him to come home on his own.

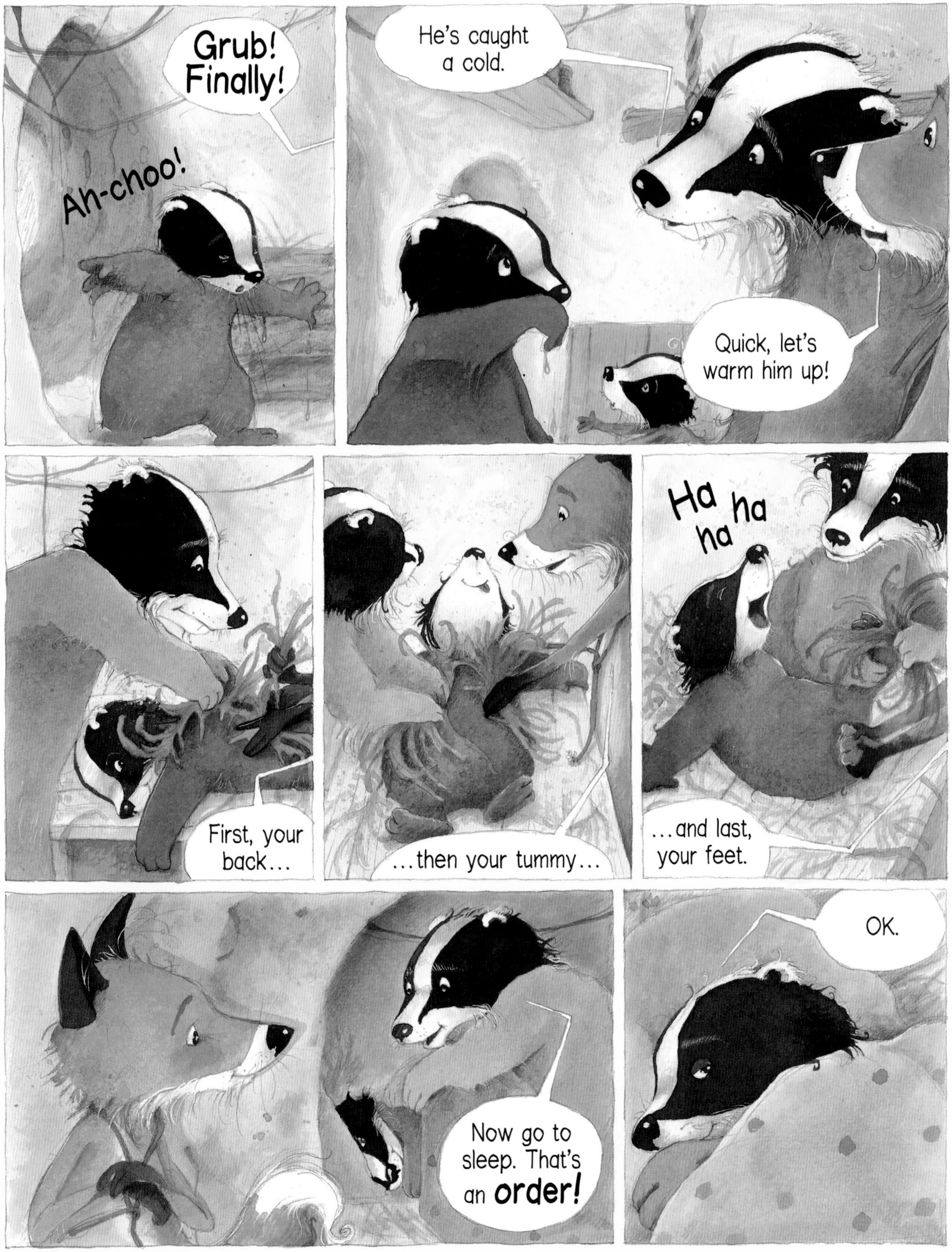
Grub! Finally!
Ah-choo!
He's caught a cold.
Quick, let's warm him up!
First, your back…
…then your tummy…
Ha ha ha
…and last, your feet.
Now go to sleep. That's an **order!**
OK.

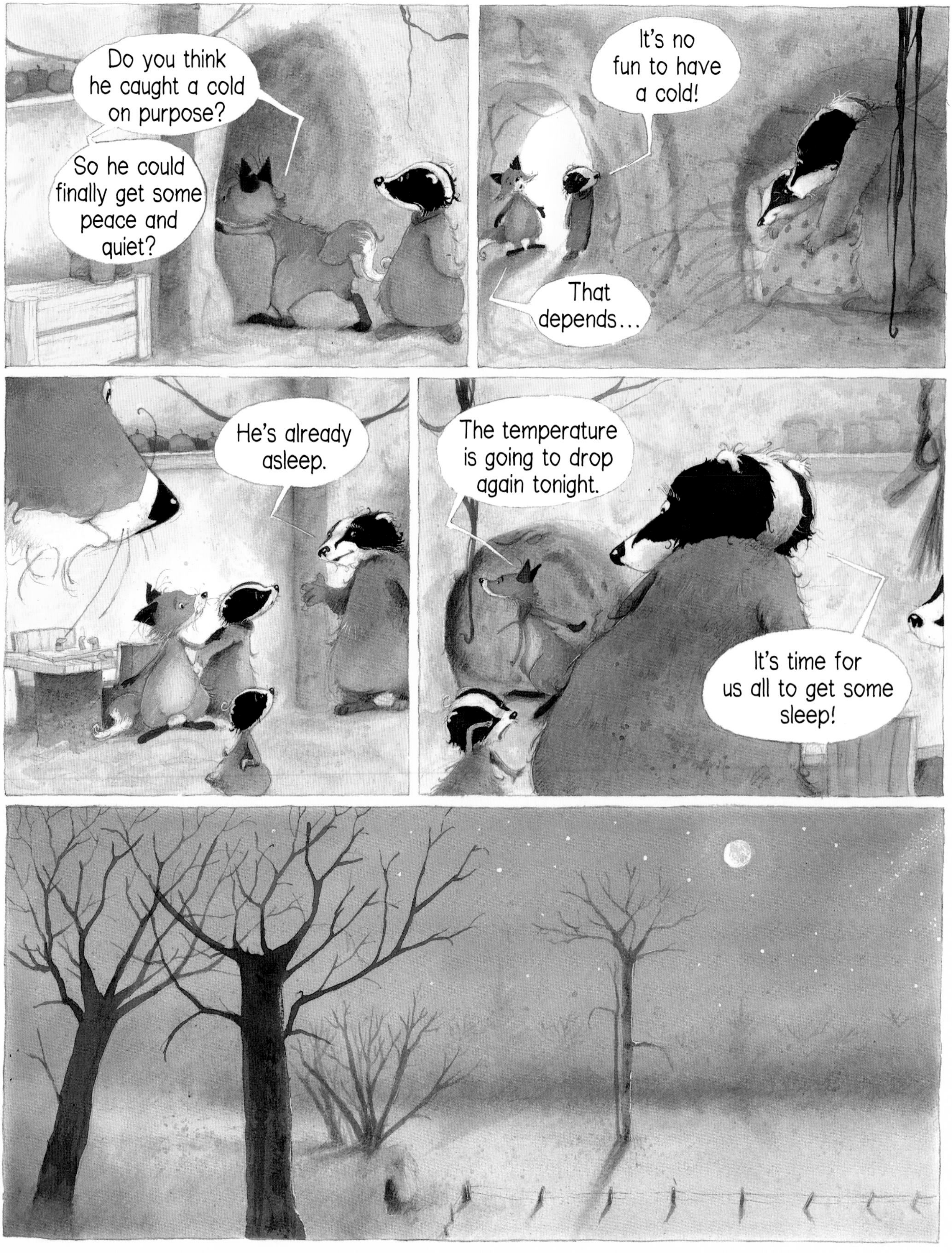
Do you think he caught a cold on purpose?
So he could finally get some peace and quiet?
It's no fun to have a cold!
That depends...
He's already asleep.
The temperature is going to drop again tonight.
It's time for us all to get some sleep!

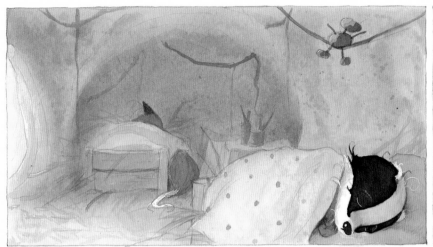

Winter is
no fun!

Come on,
Ginger!
It's time for us to
go outside.

Ooooh!
Watch me slide!
BOOM!
I'm OK!

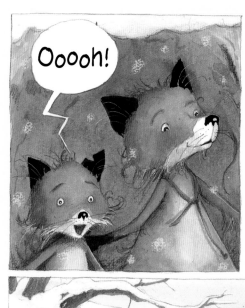

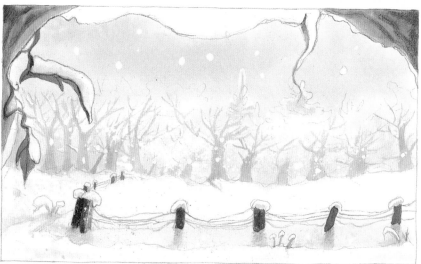

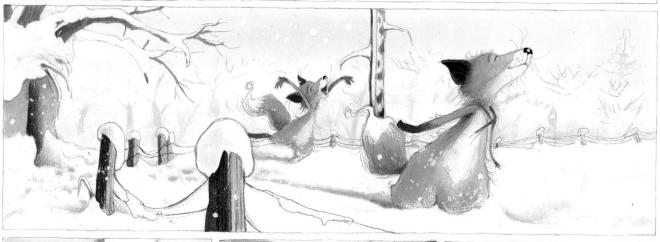

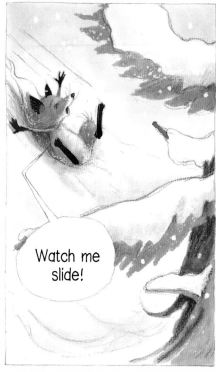

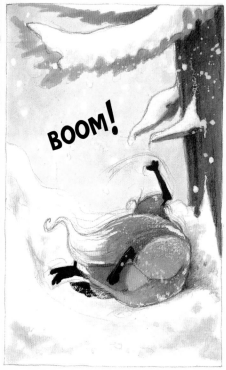

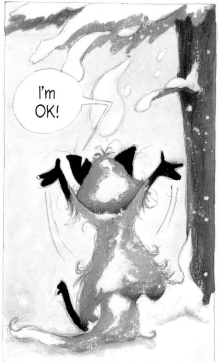

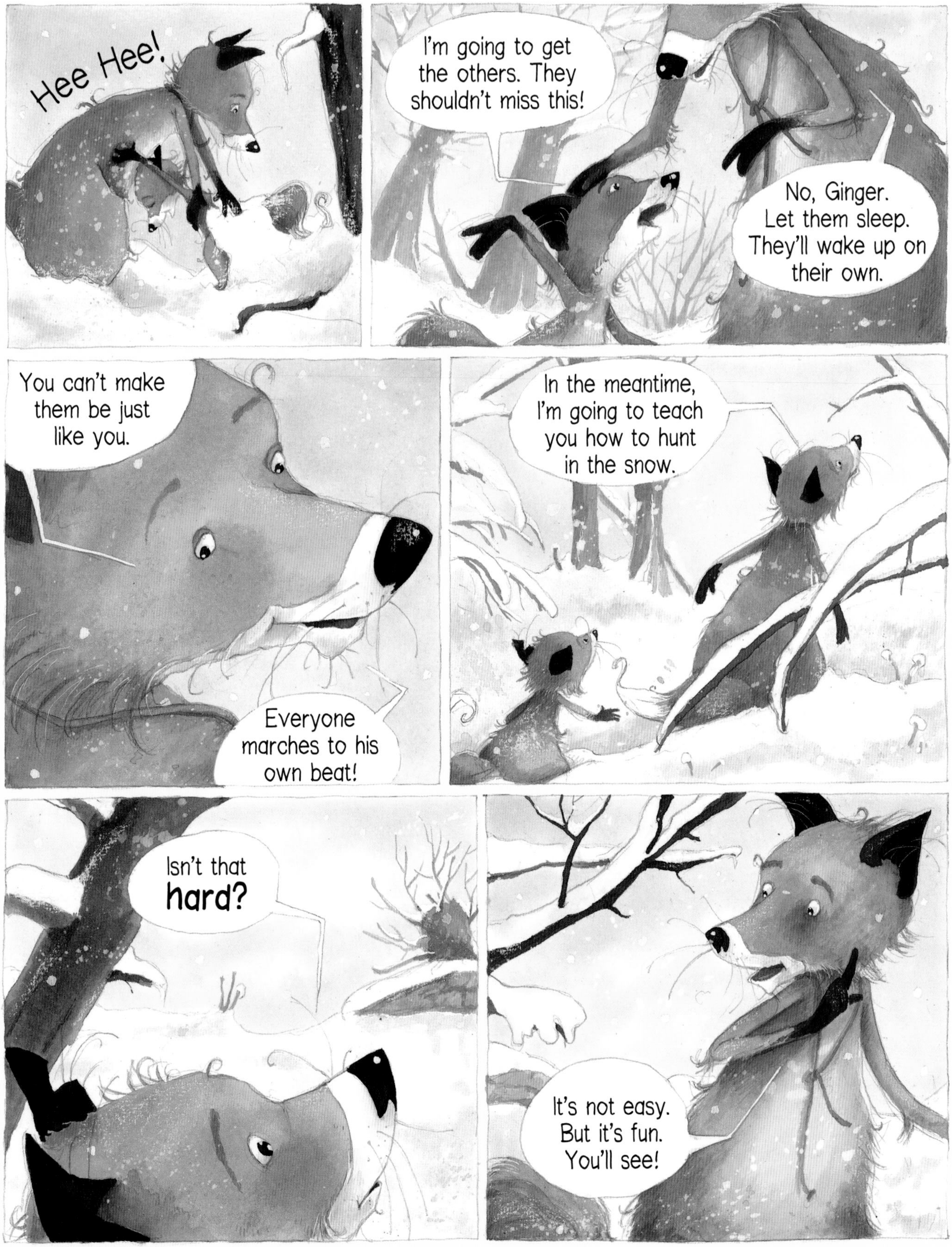
Hee Hee!
I'm going to get the others. They shouldn't miss this!
No, Ginger. Let them sleep. They'll wake up on their own.
You can't make them be just like you.
Everyone marches to his own beat!
In the meantime, I'm going to teach you how to hunt in the snow.
Isn't that **hard?**
It's not easy. But it's fun. You'll see!

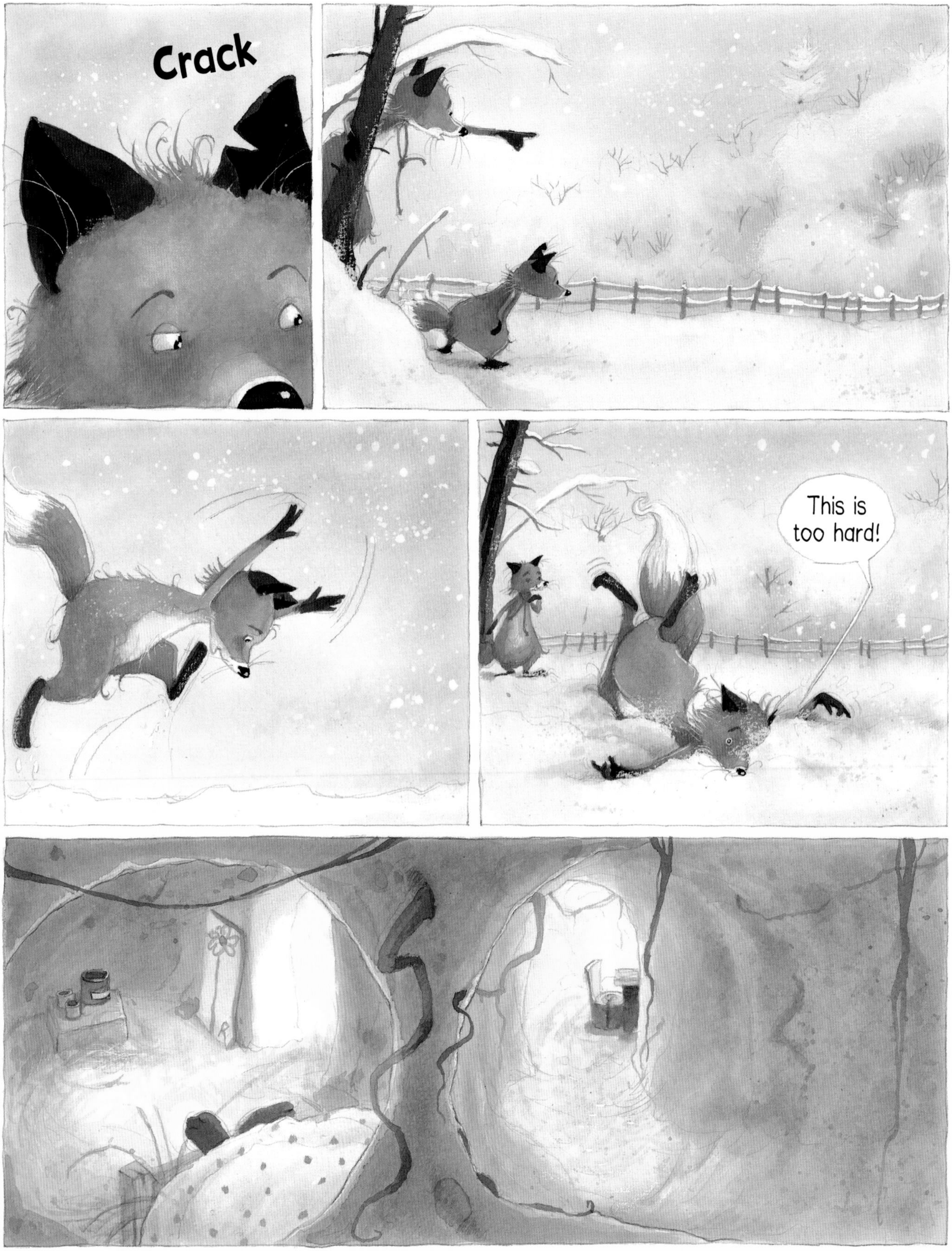
Crack
This is too hard!

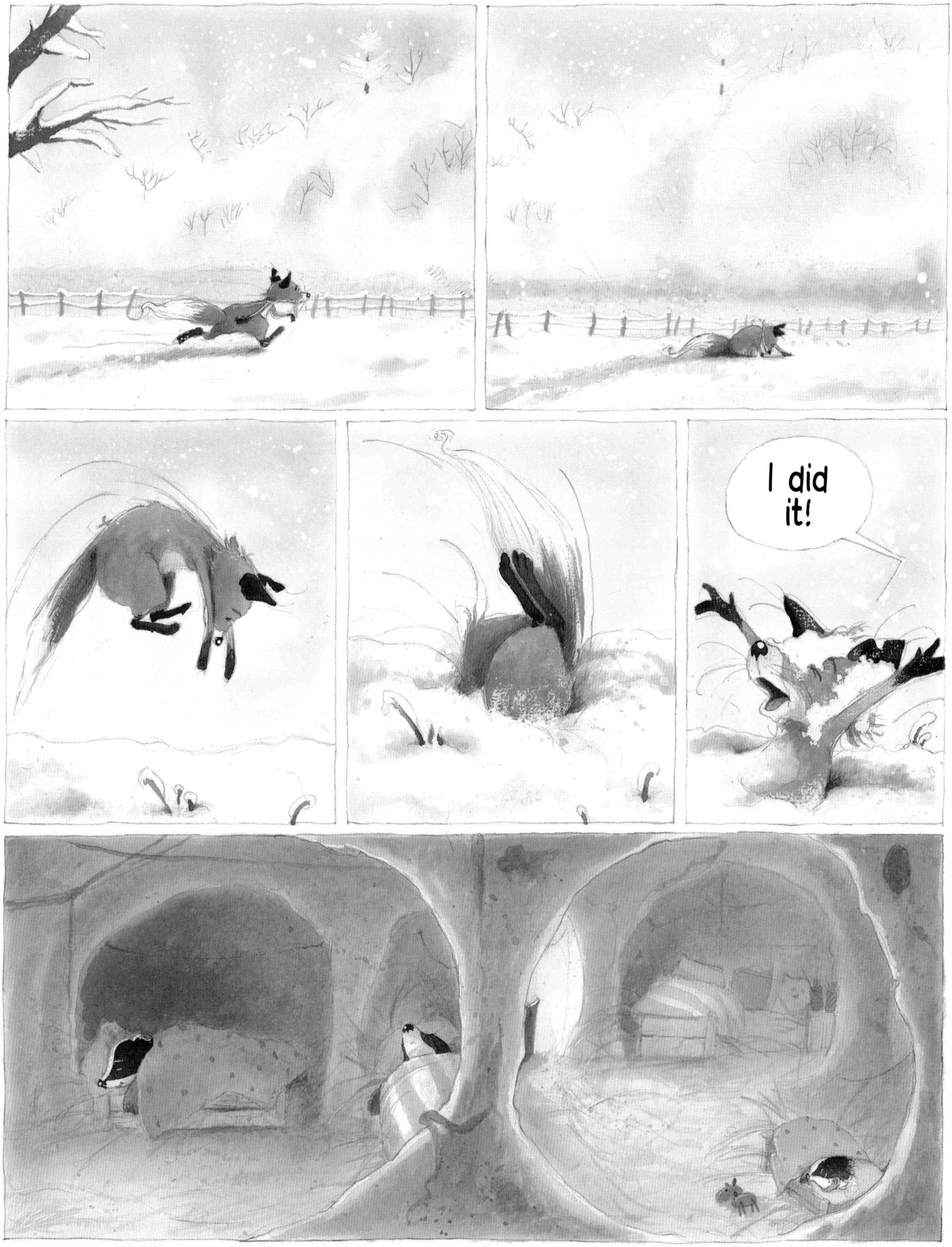
I did it!

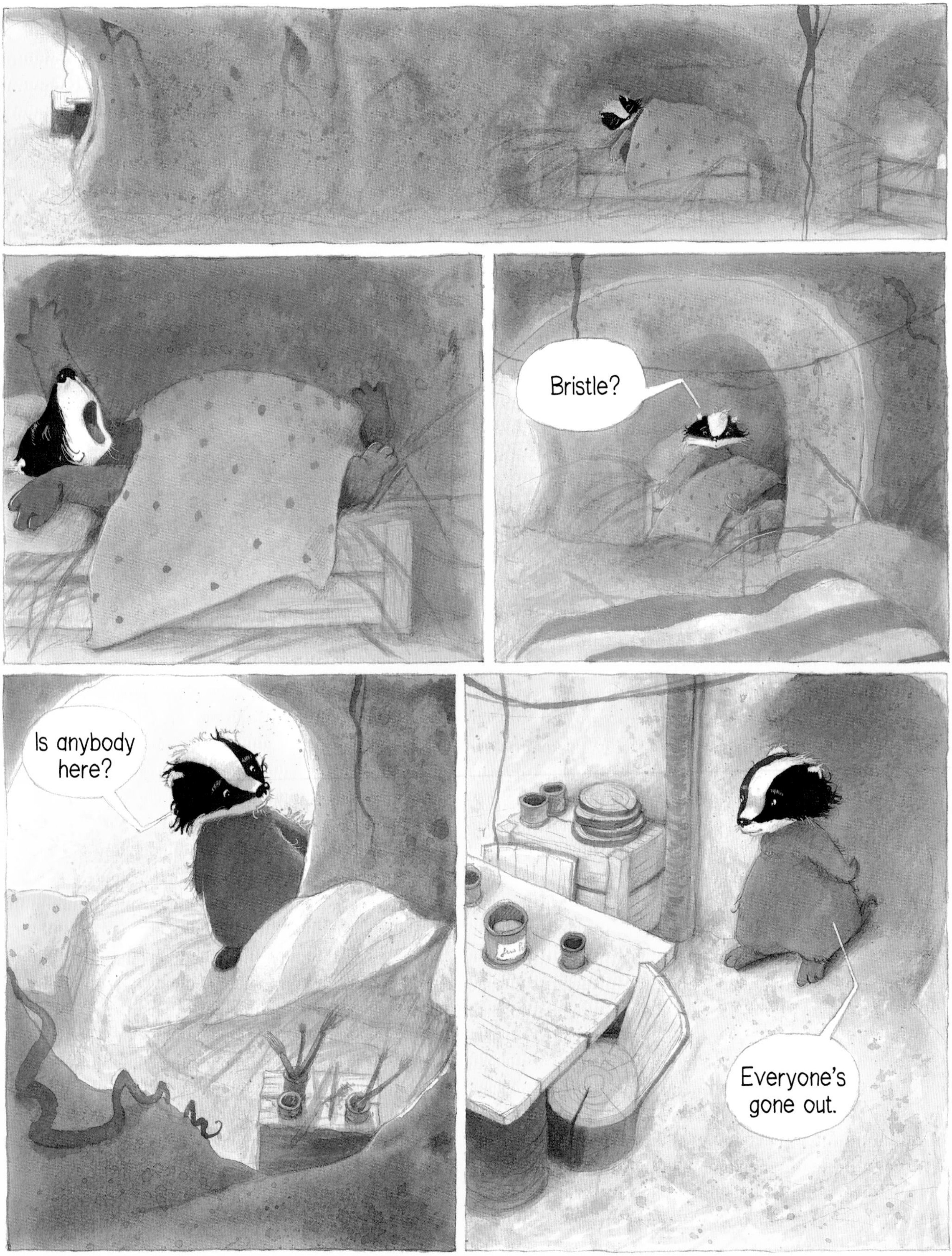

Bristle?
Is anybody here?
Everyone's gone out.

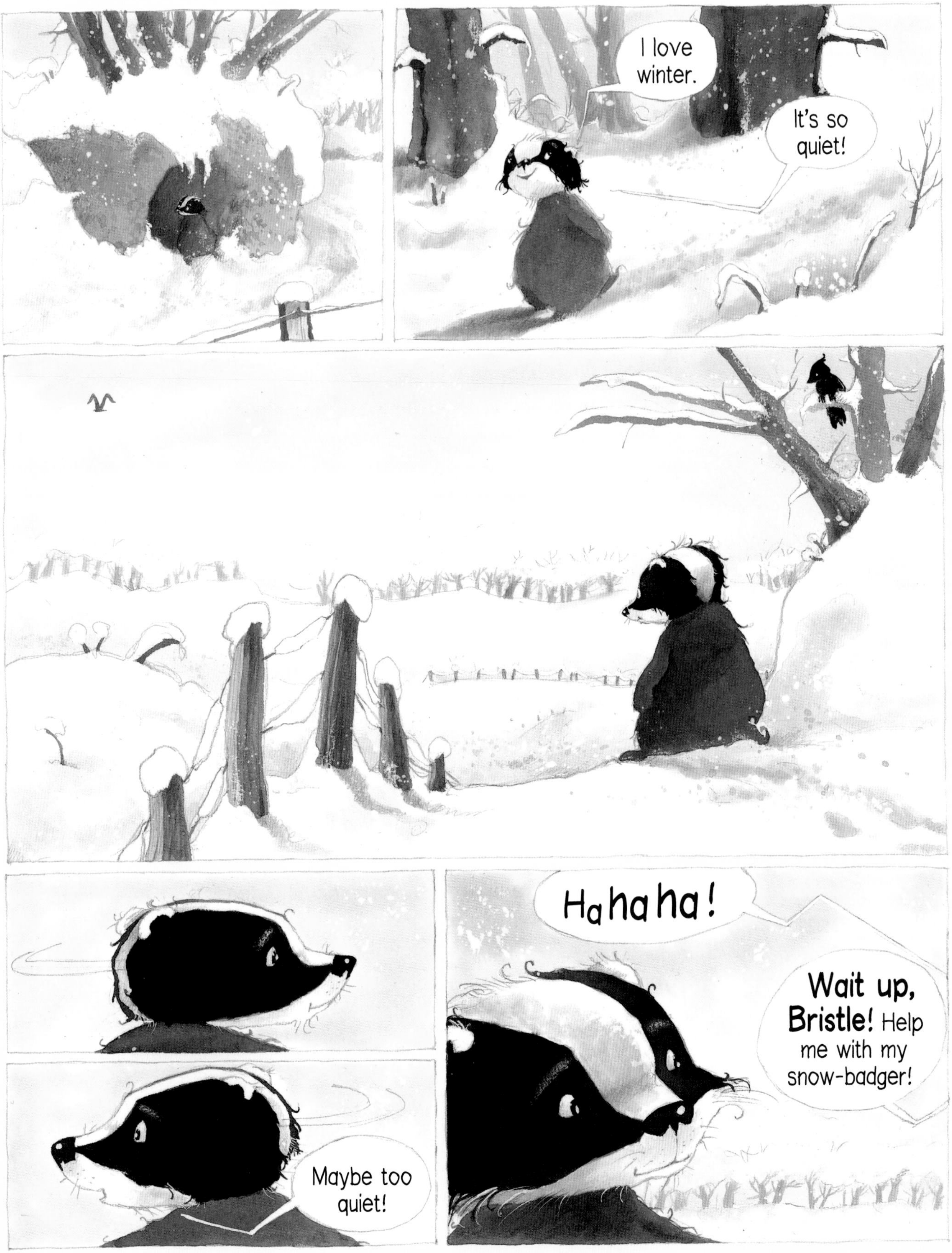

I love winter.
It's so quiet!
Maybe too quiet!
Hahaha!
Wait up, Bristle! Help me with my snow-badger!

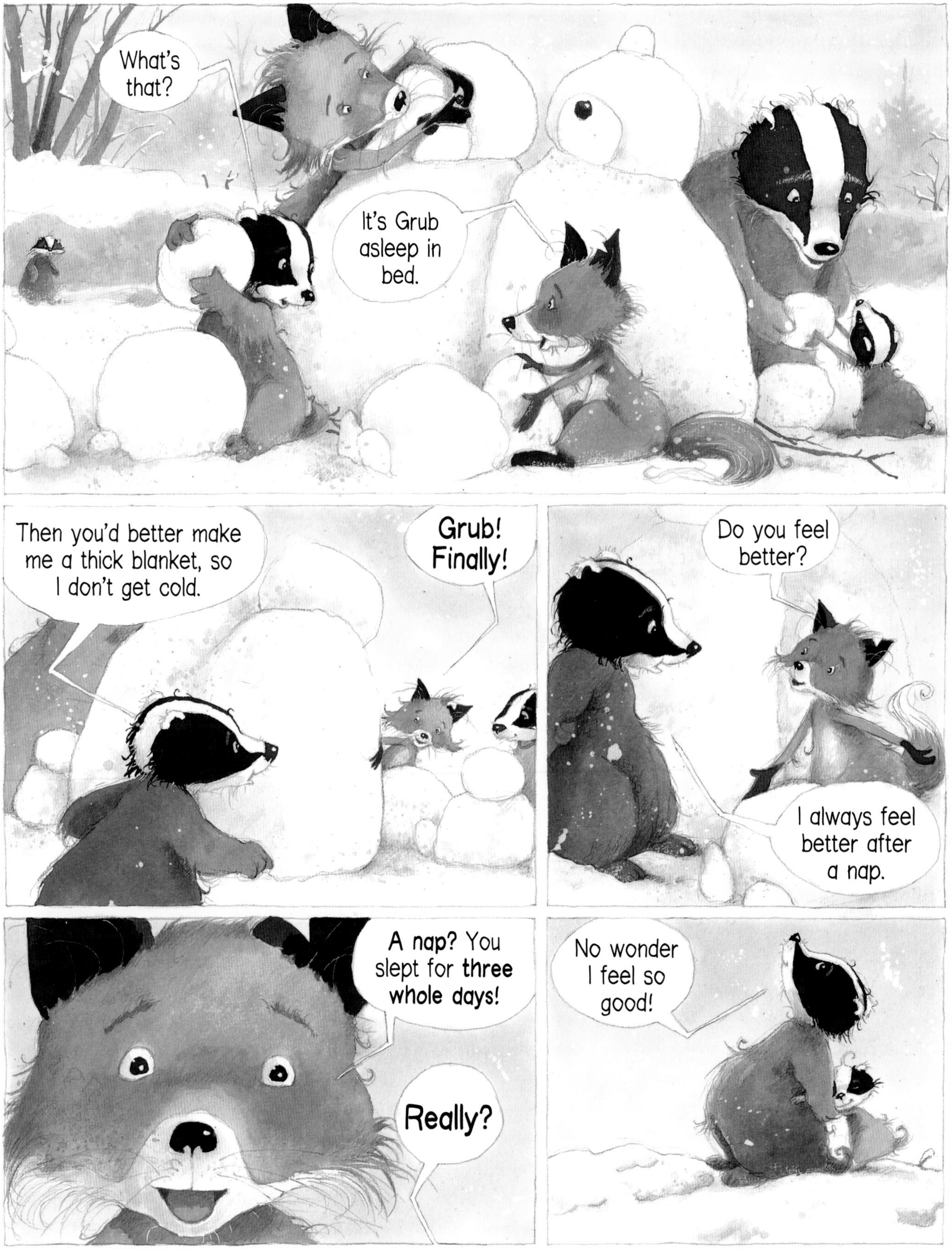

What's that?
It's Grub asleep in bed.
Then you'd better make me a thick blanket, so I don't get cold.
Grub! Finally!
Do you feel better?
I always feel better after a nap.
A nap? You slept for three whole days!
Really?
No wonder I feel so good!

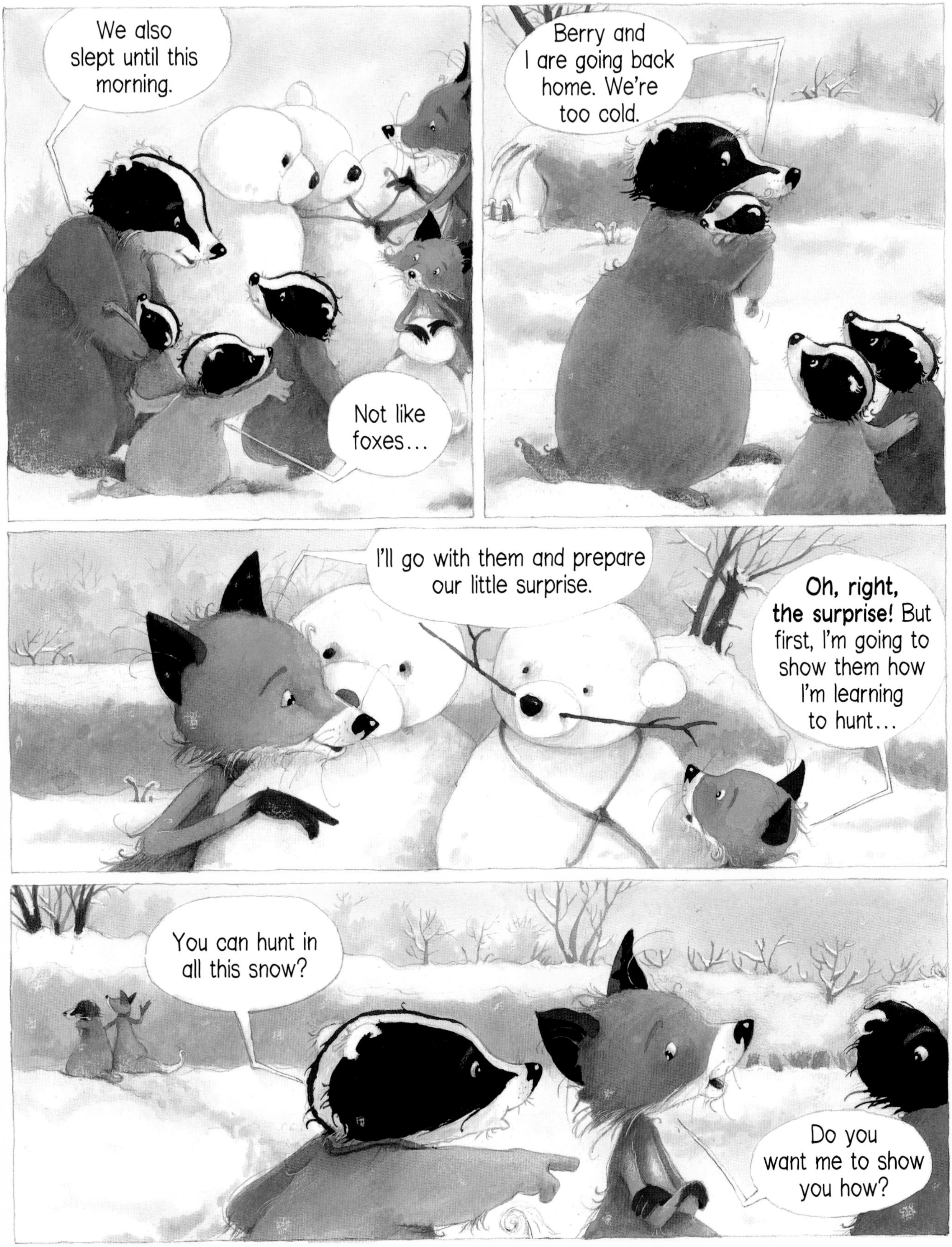
We also slept until this morning.
Not like foxes...
Berry and I are going back home. We're too cold.
I'll go with them and prepare our little surprise.
Oh, right, the surprise! But first, I'm going to show them how I'm learning to hunt...
You can hunt in all this snow?
Do you want me to show you how?

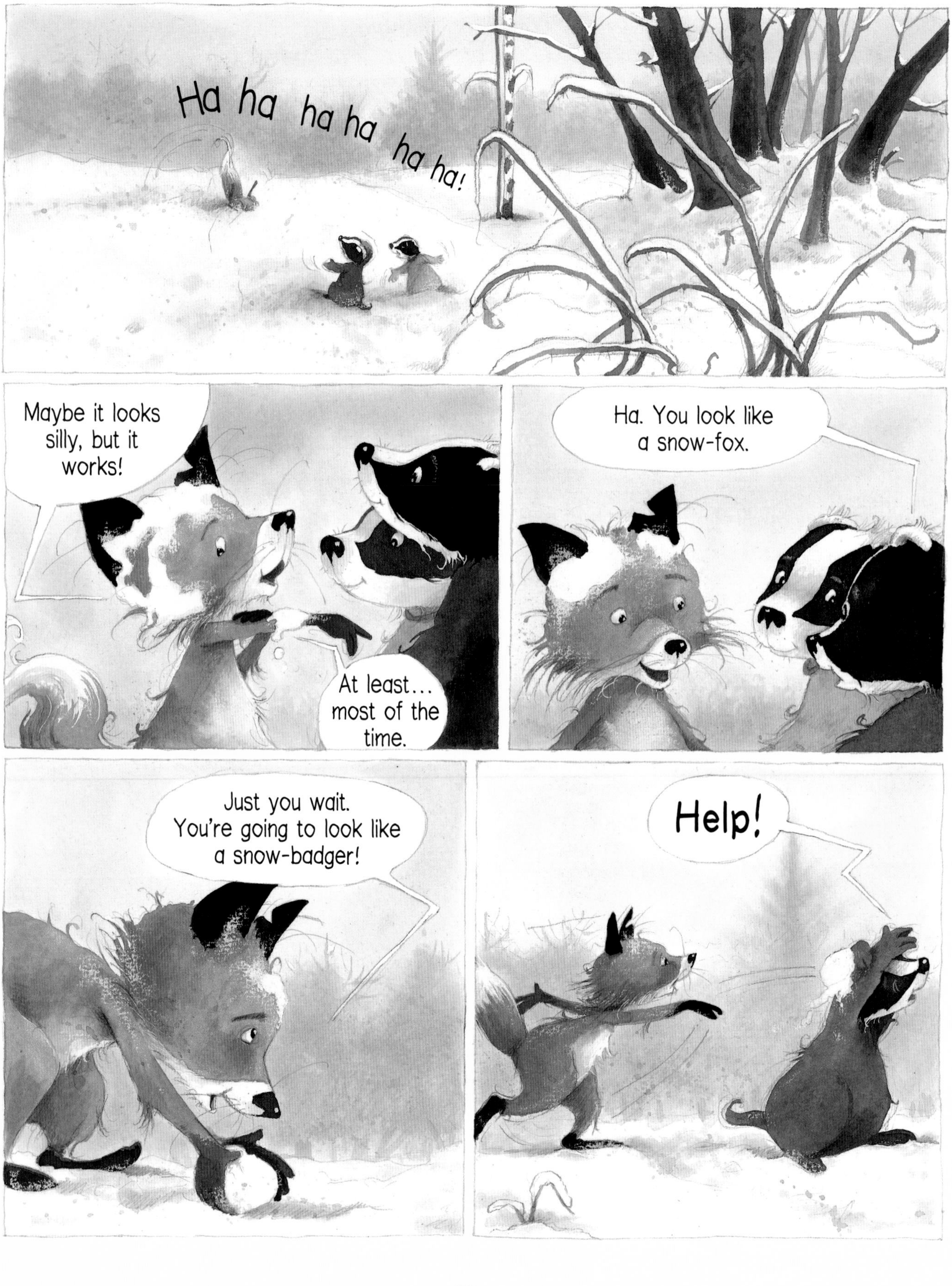
Ha ha ha ha ha ha!
Maybe it looks silly, but it works!
At least... most of the time.
Ha. You look like a snow-fox.
Just you wait. You're going to look like a snow-badger!
Help!

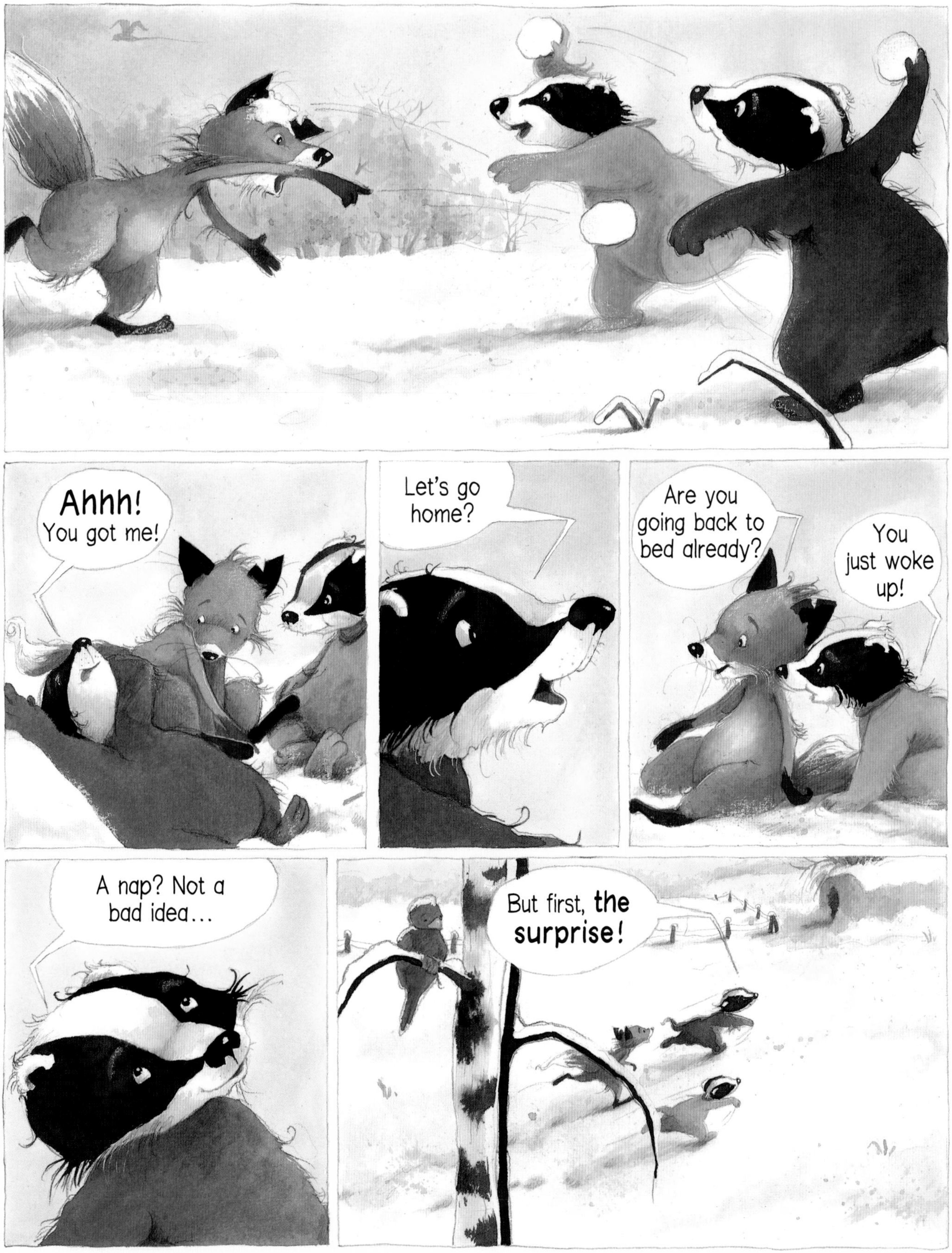
Ahhh!
You got me!
Let's go home?
Are you going back to bed already?
You just woke up!
A nap? Not a bad idea…
But first, the surprise!

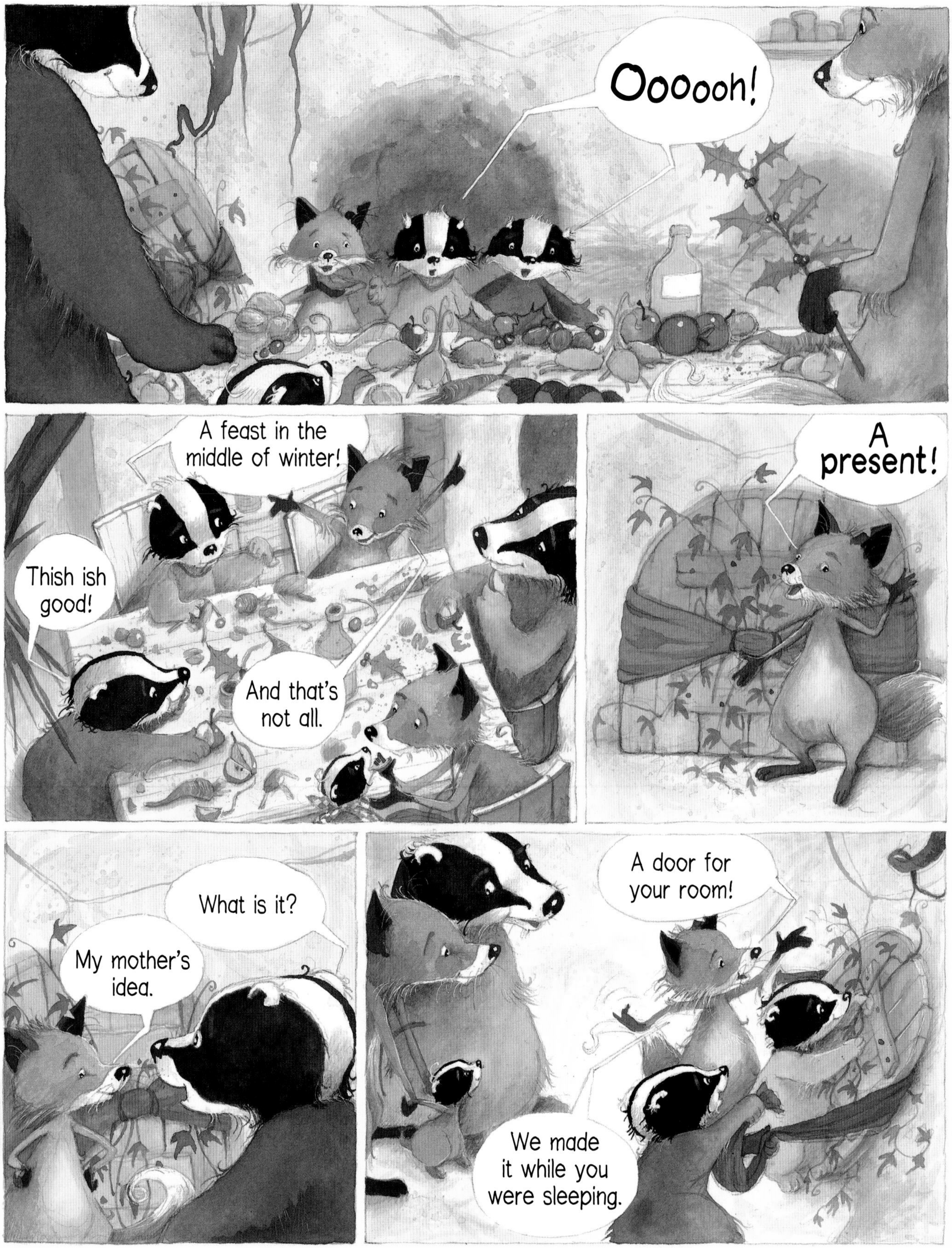
Oooooh!
A feast in the middle of winter!
Thish ish good!
And that's not all.
A present!
What is it?
My mother's idea.
A door for your room!
We made it while you were sleeping.

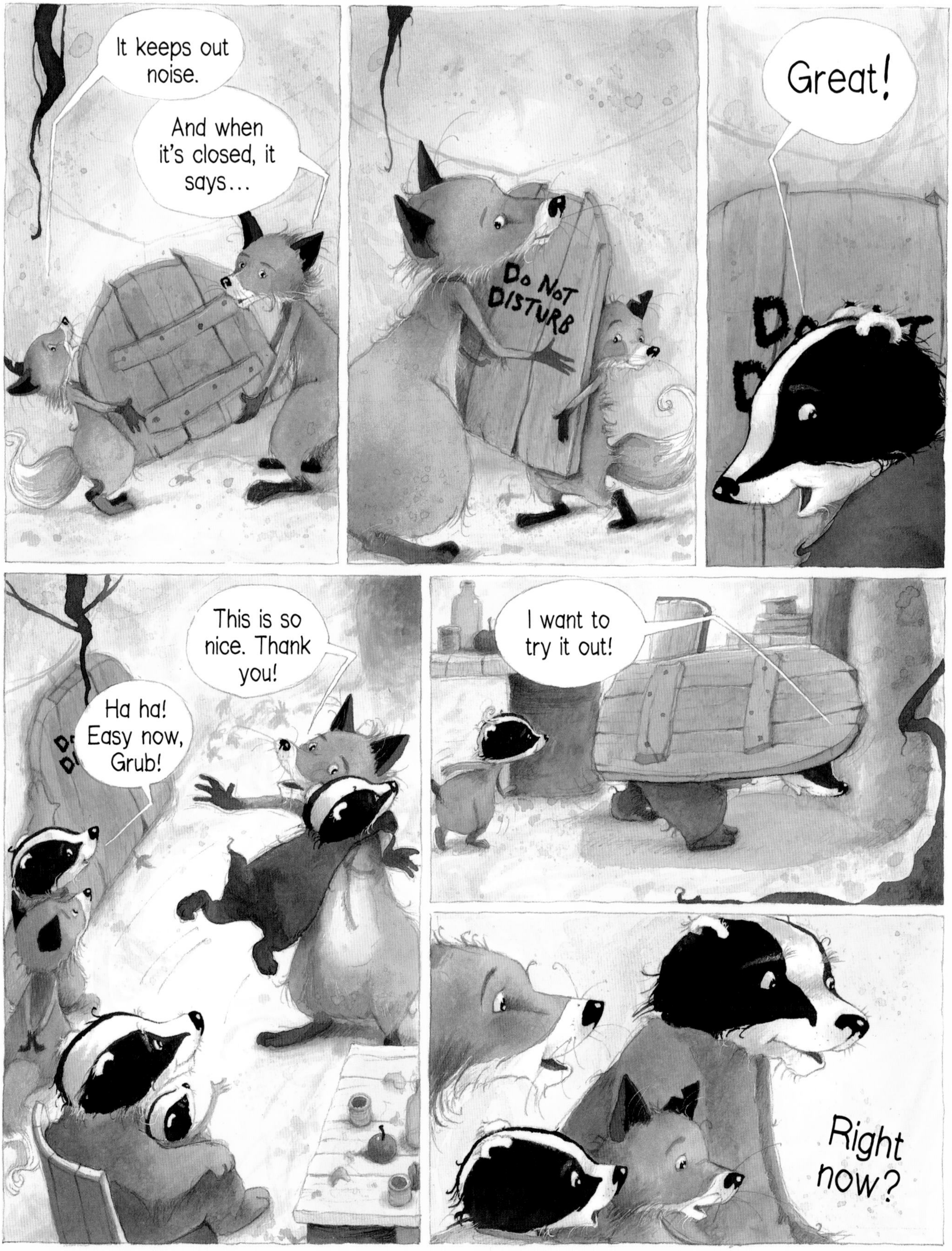
It keeps out noise.
And when it's closed, it says...
DO NOT DISTURB
Great!
This is so nice. Thank you!
Ha ha! Easy now, Grub!
I want to try it out!
Right now?

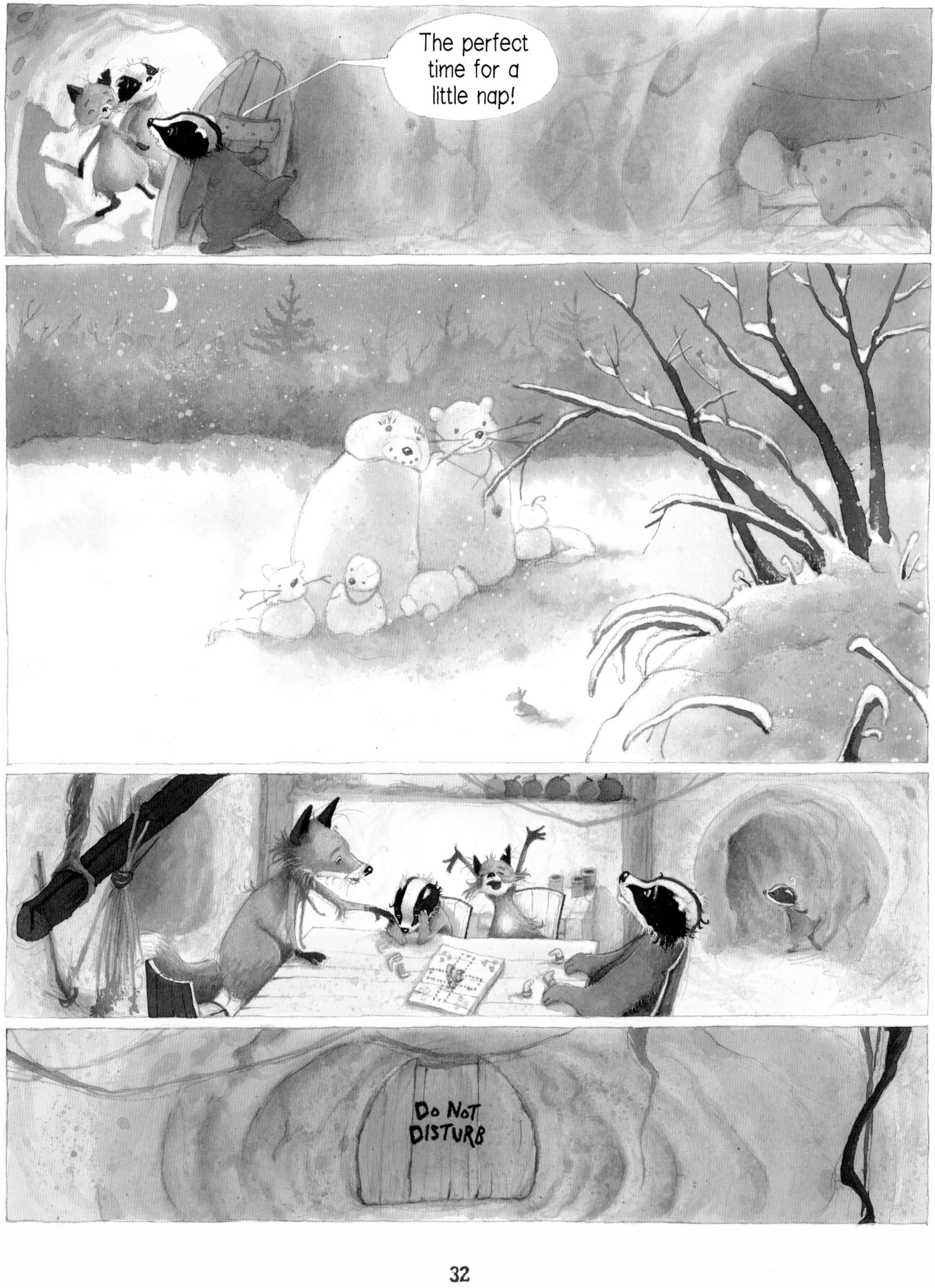
The perfect time for a little nap!
DO NOT DISTURB

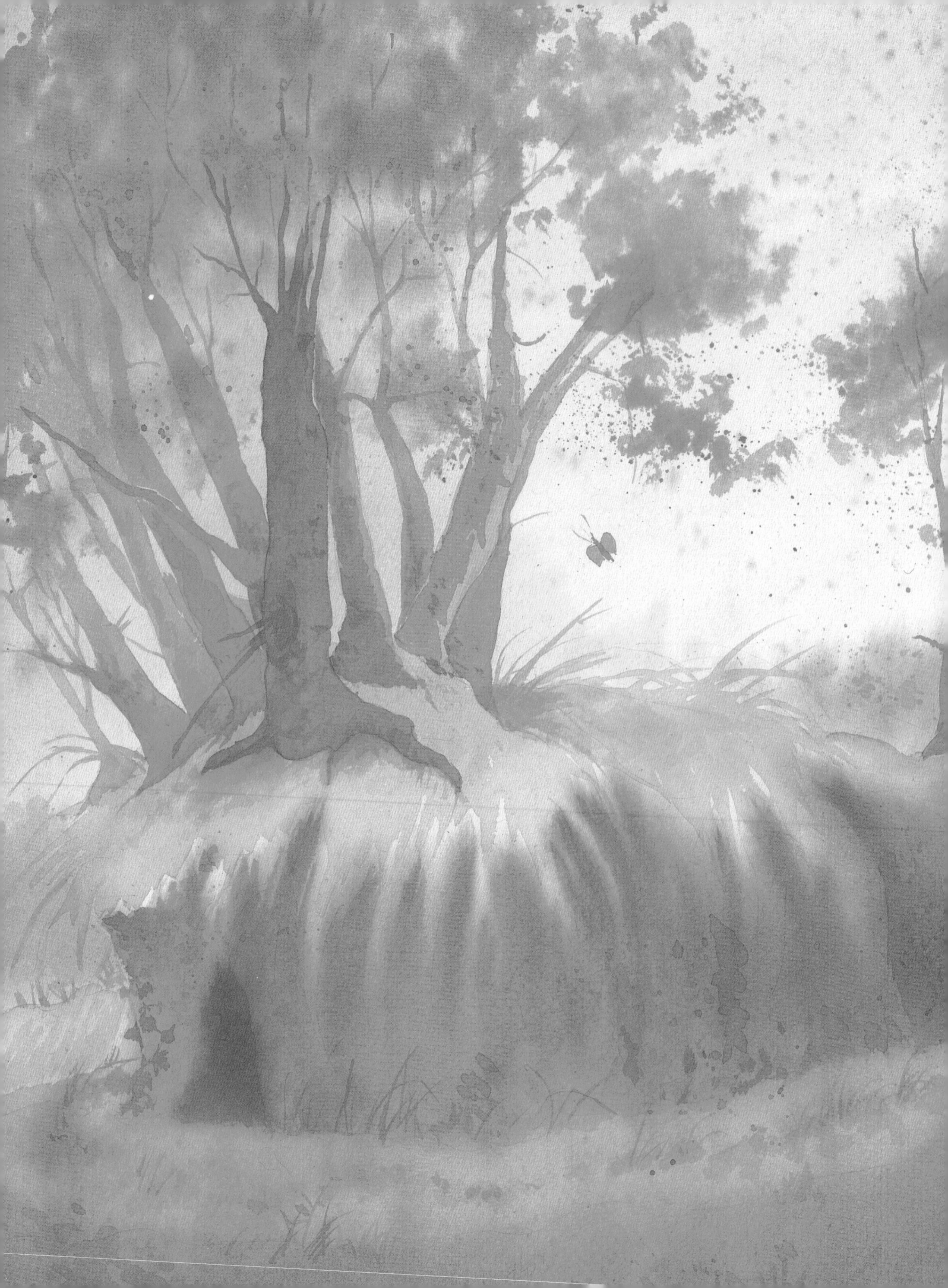